TOO TOUGH TO CARE

M. C. Millman

TOO TOUGH TO CARE

M. C. Millman

C·I·S
P·U·B·L·I·S·H·E·R·S

New York · London · Jerusalem

Published and distributed
in the U.S., Canada and overseas by
C.I.S. Publishers and Distributors
180 Park Avenue, Lakewood, New Jersey 08701
(908) 905-3000 Fax: (908) 367-6666

Distributed in Israel by
C.I.S. International (Israel)
Rechov Mishkalov 18
Har Nof, Jerusalem
Tel: 02-518-935

Distributed in the U.K. and Europe by
C.I.S. International (U.K.)
89 Craven Park Road
London N15 6AH, England
Tel: 81-809-3723

Book and cover design: Deenee Cohen
Typography: Nechamie Miller
Cover illustration: Shepsil Scheinberg

ISBN 1-56062-237-7 hardcover
1-56062-245-8 softcover
Library of Congress Catalog Card Number
93-73857

PRINTED IN THE UNITED STATES OF AMERICA

I want to acknowledge my debt to the following people without whom this book could not have come about.

- First and foremost, to my parents for the initial inspiration that set me on my way.
- To Simchah for invaluable assistance and ideas.
- To Rav Mordechai Tendler for offering *halachic* expertise on many a hypothetical situation.
- To Raizy Kaufman of C.I.S. Publishers for providing guidance and insight along the way.

"**W**HOSE MOTHER CAN HELP THE TEAM BY SEWING emblems on the new uniforms?" asked Coach Friedman.

The group of fifth-grade boys just looked at one another and shrugged.

After noticing that no one else's hand was raised, Levi Newman hesitantly raised his hand. He knew his mother was overworked, but if there were no other volunteers, he felt he might as well ask her.

"Here you go, Levi," said Coach Friedman, giving him the package of uniforms and the bag of emblems. "I think our new emblem—a star of David with a baseball in the center—is just perfect. And Levi, please send your mother thanks from the whole team. Right, guys?"

"Right, Coach," the rest of the boys responded, relieved to have found someone to do the sewing job.

Even Big Baruch, not usually given to friendly demonstrations, gave Levi what was meant to be a gentle pat on the back. It sent Levi reeling.

Levi massaged his sore back but smiled at Big Baruch nonetheless. After all, he thought, no one in his right mind wanted to get on the wrong side of Big Baruch.

Big Baruch was the team heavyweight, literally, as he was a head taller than most of the boys and at least twice as large. It was a wonder that he could walk, let alone run. But run he did, as soon as he heard the crack of the ball against the bat. More often than not, it would be a homer.

One would think that such skill would win Baruch prestige and popularity, but this wasn't so. Big Baruch was more avoided than praised. The boys tried their best to stay out of his way.

Baruch was not exactly the friendly sort himself. Any interest he displayed in others usually left them wishing he had never known they existed. In short, he was notorious for behavior more befitting a bully than a *ben Torah*.

Big Baruch watched as Levi began to lug home

the package of uniforms, the bag of emblems and his backpack full of schoolbooks. He ambled over and took the package of uniforms from Levi, leaving him with a more manageable load.

"Thanks, Baruch," Levi said appreciatively as the two boys headed for home. Levi tried to hide his discomfort with this unsolicited aid.

"I pass your house on my way home anyway," Big Baruch said gruffly. "Are you sure your mom won't mind sewing all these uniforms?"

"Actually," Levi answered sheepishly, "I'm not even sure she'll be able to do it. She's been awfully busy at work lately. Usually, she's too tired after a hard day to even manage all the stuff around the house. But it looks like none of the other guys' mothers even have sewing machines. At least we've got that."

"Yeah?" Baruch replied, perplexed. "Well, what good is a sewing machine with no one to run it?"

"I'll manage something," retorted Levi evasively, sorry for having said so much. "Maybe she'll end up having some extra time this week after all."

"And if not, then what?" Baruch prodded. "The whole team is counting on you to get the uniforms done, you know."

"Don't worry, Baruch," replied Levi. "If worse comes to worse, I'll just have to do it myself," he added half-jokingly, looking nervously over his shoulder to check if anyone else might be near enough to have heard.

Baruch put down his bundle and looked at Levi in obvious surprise.

"You mean you know how to use a sewing machine?" he asked.

"Whatever," Levi replied shortly. "I'll manage something."

Presently, they arrived at Levi's front door. Levi thanked Baruch for his help, and they put the uniforms and emblems down inside the door.

"Hope you get it all done," Baruch called over his shoulder, "however you work it out."

Levi closed the door, letting out a sigh of relief as he watched Baruch's retreating figure through the window.

That was close, he said to himself. Since when is Big Baruch so friendly, anyway?

Levi suspected that his image would not exactly be helped if the boys knew about his ability to sew!

"Levi's home! Levi's home!" called a voice.

"Hi, Chaim." Levi scooped up his three-year-old brother and whirled him around. "Where's Mom?"

"In the kitchen," Chaim answered.

Levi left his things near the front door and headed for the kitchen to speak to his mother. She looked quite frazzled. Sunday was her one afternoon off from teaching at the girls' high school, so she usually spent it cooking meals for the rest of the week. Right then, she was stirring the contents of a pot while balancing a variety of seasonings in her other hand. She put down the spoon with a clatter, only to remove the lid from another pot to check its contents.

"Oh, Levi," she said, glancing up from her work. "Hello, dear, how was your day?"

"Fine, thanks, Mom," Levi replied. "I was just wondering if you needed any help with anything? Maybe you want me to wash the dishes, or take the kids out, or something." He wanted to get on her good side before asking any favors.

"Well, actually, maybe you would like to . . ." She glanced at him sharply. "What do you need from me, Levi? I know your style when you're about to ask a favor."

"Well, since you put it that way . . ." Levi began nervously.

He was interrupted by a cry from Chaim.

"What's wrong, Chaim?" Mrs. Newman asked.

"I bumped my toe!" Chaim wailed.

"Come here and let me see," Levi beckoned.

Chaim climbed onto Levi's lap. Levi took off Chaim's sock to examine his foot while Chaim bent over to get a look himself.

"I don't see anything," Levi said as he put Chaim's sock back on.

"That's because it's the other foot," Chaim said, tugging off the other sock to help Levi check his hurt foot.

"Chaim," said Mrs. Newman with a laugh, "if your foot is better, why don't you go play in the family room for a little while?" Chaim skipped off Levi's lap and left the room.

"Now, Levi," she continued, "what was it you were saying?"

"Well," said Levi. "You see, Mom, we were the only family on the whole team with a sewing machine. So we get to sew the emblems onto the team uniforms."

"That's fine," his mother replied, walking over to peek in the oven. "You must be glad you learned how to sew. I'm sure the whole team appreciates your offer."

"Well, actually, Mom . . ." This was going to be harder than Levi had thought. "I was hoping you could maybe find a little time to do it for me? I'll do whatever else you need around the house, if only you'll just do some of the sewing."

"Whatever do you mean, Levi? I thought you enjoyed sewing. I'm sure you're skilled enough to be able to handle something as simple as sewing emblems onto the team uniforms. It can't be that complicated now, can it?"

Levi looked down at his feet. How could he explain how sure he was that he would be teased mercilessly if the guys found out about his sewing skills?

His mother looked at his downcast eyes. Perhaps Levi is just as busy as I am, she thought.

Hadn't he mentioned just last week that he had a huge, comprehensive *Mishnayos* test? She couldn't remember when it was going to be, but it probably was coming soon.

"It's that *Mishnayos* test you have coming up, isn't it?" she asked.

"What?" asked Levi. "No, that's not for a while. Why?"

"Then what's the problem with doing the sewing yourself?" she asked, utterly stumped.

Then she remembered that when Levi had first taken an interest in learning to sew, he had insisted that he was only doing it to help out around the house and that he absolutely didn't want anyone else to know. She had felt that his qualms about what people would think were unjustified. This could be the perfect time to show him just that.

"I'm sorry, Levi," she said after the momentary pause, "but you really picked the wrong week to volunteer my time. I'm afraid I just won't be able to manage it, even if you help me with other things around the house. I really am sorry, dear, but I know you'll come through just fine without me."

She turned back to her cooking with an air of finality that made it clear that the conversation had come to an end.

Levi left the kitchen with mounting desperation. Now what? he thought. If he did it himself, what would happen when Coach would ask the team to thank his mother personally for her time? Would she try to set the record straight, or would she agree not to mention his sewing ability?

Levi knew he couldn't let the team down. He would sew the emblems himself, and he would just have to think of a way to avoid mention of where credit for the sewing really belonged. He decided to start on the first emblem as soon as he finished his homework.

As the sewing machine whirred, Levi came up with what seemed to be a brilliant plan. After turning over the uniforms to Coach Friedman, he would just take him aside and explain that his mother was shy and very humble. It would simply embarrass her if they tried to thank her. He was sure Coach would understand. Levi would even promise to tell his mother himself just how grateful the team was. After all, Levi told himself, my mother really is a bit shy, not to mention humble, so I wouldn't really be saying anything that isn't true.

Of course, things did not work out quite as smoothly as Levi had planned.

LEVI HAD THE UNIFORMS READY FOR THE TEAM'S next practice. However, before he managed to have a private word with Coach Friedman, everyone came crowding around to check out the new uniform emblems.

"Looks good," said Mordechai, Levi's best friend, as he examined a few samples.

The other boys murmured in agreement. Those in the back pushed closer to get a better view, almost knocking Coach Friedman off his feet. Coach Friedman decided it would be best to pass out the uniforms immediately.

"Okay, team," Coach Friedman called out. "Line up over here, and I'll start handing out the uniforms. No pushing, please. Right behind Dovid here."

The boys lined up, and each was handed a uniform of the appropriate size.

"Wow," Shimmy said excitedly. "The team emblem really looks great!"

"Okay if we try it on now, Coach?" Dovid asked.

"Go ahead, and let's see how they look," Coach Friedman agreed as he passed out the last uniform.

"Uh, Coach, could I speak to you for a moment about the uniforms?" Levi asked, seizing what looked like the perfect opportunity to make his speech. "You see, my mother . . ."

"Hey, Coach, something's wrong over here!" one of the boys called out.

Coach Friedman and Levi both looked over to where most of the boys were parading around in their new uniforms. Two boys appeared to be having difficulty getting the shirts on over their heads.

"What's going on here?" asked one muffled voice. "I think my uniform is too small."

"My head can't even fit through this," another muffled voice stated.

"Coach, I'm stuck," called out a voice that sounded like Dovid's. "Get me out of here! I have claustrophobia. Help, someone, I'm stuck!"

Coach Friedman was at the boy's side in three quick strides. "I'll have you out of here in a moment," he said, trying to tug the shirt down where it belonged.

"This isn't going to work," he added shortly. Instead, he pulled the uniform off, unwrapping Dovid from the mess in which he had managed to entangle himself.

"Thanks," said Dovid breathlessly.

"I'm coming," Coach Friedman called to the next covered figure, who was turning circles helplessly while trying to extricate himself from his uniform.

The identity of the trapped boy was obvious to everyone from the sheer bulk of the figure and the loudness of the grunts coming from somewhere deep inside the material.

"That's got to be Big Baruch," Mordechai said grimly.

Levi looked on with growing horror.

Suddenly, Coach Friedman realized what had happened. It seemed that some of the emblems had not only been strongly attached to the front of the uniform, but had been stitched straight through to the back side as well.

When all the team members were disentangled, the whole group began to close in on Levi, Big Baruch nearest of all.

"What's the big idea, Levi?" Dovid called out.

"Yeah, we thought these were supposed to be

sewn by someone who knew what she was doing," added Shimmy.

"Maybe this is Levi's idea of a joke," Shmully suggested.

"Some joke all right," Big Baruch growled.

Levi felt Coach Friedman's hand grip his shoulder. His other hand held the offending uniforms. To Levi, the coach's hand on his shoulder felt like a ton of bricks, but he couldn't think of any way to escape Coach's hold. Also, he knew he wouldn't get too far with Big Baruch glowering at him, just inches away.

"Your mother didn't sew these after all," Baruch shouted accusingly, his face still red and sweaty from the struggle to disentangle himself from the uniform. "I bet you sewed these yourself, didn't you, Newman? Who else would make such a mistake? You'll pay for it, too, in more ways than one. For starters, I expect a new uniform, of course."

It was quite obvious that Big Baruch had more than a new uniform in mind from the way his fists kept clenching and unclenching while he spoke.

"Really, it's no big deal," said Levi, holding up his hands as if to stop the onslaught of words and the unspoken threats. "The stitches can easily be pulled out and redone properly."

"So, you admit it," Big Baruch said triumphantly. "You are the one who did the sewing."

"And a fine job of it, too," Coach Friedman

broke in, "whoever it was."

He pointed to the emblem on another boy's uniform, which had been attached properly.

"Anyone can make a mistake," Mordechai voiced his opinion in defense of his friend.

"There's mistakes and there's mistakes," Dovid grumbled, unimpressed with Mordechai's statement and still embarrassed by his own panicky display while entangled in the uniform.

"Levi has already said that he doesn't think it will be a problem to fix it," Coach Friedman stated soothingly.

"Of course not," Levi affirmed. "They can be redone by our next practice."

"Why are we all standing around, then?" asked Shmully.

"Yeah," added Mordechai. "We've wasted enough time already. Levi says he'll get them fixed, so let's play ball already."

"Okay, boys, let's start those warm-ups," Coach called out, pleased that order had been restored.

Levi heaved a sigh of relief and went to put the two offending uniforms into his backpack to take home. He then joined the rest of the boys for their pre-game warm-ups.

"Thanks for standing up for me," he whispered to Mordechai as they jogged in place.

"No problem," Mordechai replied. "But I don't think you've seen the end of this yet."

He motioned behind them to where Big Baruch

was jogging in place and glaring fiercely in Levi's direction.

"What rotten luck," Levi said in a whisper. "Of all people to have gotten one of those uniforms!"

"Looks to me like you're in trouble," said Mordechai sympathetically. "I don't think he's the type to forget it all by tomorrow."

The next day, their suspicions were confirmed as Levi and Mordechai wove their way through the packed hallway towards class.

"Hey, watch out!" called Mordechai, but it was already too late.

An unmistakable figure barreled out of the crowd and bumped right into Levi.

"Are you all right?" asked several boys who quickly gathered around Levi.

"Who was that, anyway?" asked another.

"Big Baruch, who else?" answered Mordechai.

"You'd better be careful, Levi," called out another boy. "He's out to get you for sure. I wouldn't want to be in your shoes."

"I wouldn't either," replied Levi miserably.

The boys nodded sympathetically. They all shared a common fear of Big Baruch's unwanted attention.

"Come on," said Mordechai, giving Levi's arm a tug. "Let's get ready for class. We'll just keep a lookout for him, that's all."

The next day, Big Baruch struck again, this time in the classroom.

"Watch it!" Mordechai suddenly exclaimed in a hoarse whisper.

This time, Levi narrowly avoided Big Baruch, who just happened to feel the need to push back his chair and stretch out his arms at exactly the moment Levi came up the aisle to hand in his test paper.

"Sorry," said Big Baruch in a tone that said he was anything but sorry. Levi understood that Big Baruch had no intention of letting him off the hook, and he was afraid.

THIS IS IT," LEVI THOUGHT. "NOW I'M REALLY going to get it."

His heart was pounding so loudly that he could barely hear himself think.

Big Baruch had managed to corner Levi on the playground during recess. His fist gripped Levi's collar so tightly that Levi had to stand on his toes to free his throat enough to breathe.

Levi waited for the first blows to fall, but they never did. Instead, to his surprise, Big Baruch's booming voice took on an almost pleading tone.

"You've got to help me, Newman," said Big

Baruch. "You're my only hope. I've got to be somewhere important this afternoon. My father is taking me to meet his *rosh yeshivah*, and I'm obviously in no shape as things are! I tore my pants this morning, and there's no way I can meet the *rosh yeshivah* in this condition."

Abruptly, he released his grip on Levi. Caught unaware, Levi landed on the ground with a re-sounding thud. Big Baruch seemed not to notice. He turned around, revealing a split in his pants. It was clear that Big Baruch's pants would have served him better a size or so larger.

Levi stood up and dusted off the seat of his own pants. He wasn't quite sure what Big Baruch wanted of him, but he had to tread carefully lest that hand close around his collar again. He cautiously backed away a few steps before answering.

"So, how can I help you, Baruch?" he asked in as polite a tone as he could manage.

Baruch rolled his eyes. "Your sewing machine, that's what. I told you, I have to be somewhere important right after school. You've got to help me fix this. Now!"

Levi took a few more steps backwards, his eyes roaming the playground to see if any help was near, perhaps in the form of some heaven-sent *rebbe* strolling nearby. But it seemed luck was not with him.

"But Baruch, we can't just pick up and leave during school," Levi objected. "What will Reb

Hirsh say, not to mention the principal or my parents when they hear about it?" He fingered his collar nervously.

"No problem," declared Baruch. "We'll slip out during lunch. No one will ever miss us."

And so, instead of spending his lunch hour enjoying his tuna sandwich on fresh rye bread with a crunchy dill pickle, Levi found himself bent over his sewing machine, mending Big Baruch's pants.

"Why do you look so worried, Newman?" asked Baruch, leaning over to examine Levi's work. "Is a job like this too hard for you?"

"Don't worry, Baruch. I can handle a simple job like this. I'm just worried about us leaving school. I sure hope no one misses us, you know?"

"Just keep your mind on your work," Baruch replied. "No one's going to care if you skip a lunch hour once in your life."

"Probably not," said Levi, taking out a scissors to cut off the hanging threads. "Well, it's done. How does it look?"

"Looks fine . . . if you didn't sew the legs together or something," Baruch replied suspiciously. He slipped the pants on. "Feels fine too, Newman. How am I going to repay you?"

"Don't worry about it," said Levi quickly. "Just chalk it up as a double *chesed*. I got the chance to save both our skins at once," he added with a hint of sarcasm.

"Okay," said Baruch. "But why you want to keep your talent a secret, I sure don't understand," he added, thumping Levi on the back in a friendly fashion.

Levi stumbled from the force of the blow but managed to recover both his balance and his composure quickly. Could it be, he thought, that Baruch was actually trying to be nice? If so, it was difficult to tell his friendly style from his angry one.

"Hey, Newman!" said Baruch as they headed back to school. "Do me a favor and don't mention this whole business with my pants to anyone. Okay?"

"Sure, Baruch, no problem." Levi was only too glad to agree.

4

THE LUNCH ROOM WAS STILL FULL WHEN THE boys returned. Levi stopped at the drinking fountain while Baruch went into their classroom. The doors of the lunch room were soon thrown open, and a stream of chattering boys flowed into the hall.

"Hey, wait up," Levi called as he spotted Mordechai and Shmully walking toward the classroom.

Shmully was the friendly, but rather dull type who often attached himself to one or another of his classmates. They, in turn, tolerated his presence, though most didn't go to great lengths to include him in their plans. Shmully never seemed to notice or mind.

"Where were you during lunch?" Mordechai asked as Levi fell into step beside them.

"I wouldn't worry about that now," Levi replied evasively, remembering his promise to Big Baruch. "I think we should put our minds in high gear for whatever math problem Mr. Simons has in store for us."

"Yeah," agreed Shmully glumly. "He said this time we would even be using the computers. His old problems were tough enough, and now he wants us to use the computers? How am I ever going to figure out the answers to his math problems when he complicates things with computers?"

Levi and Mordechai nodded sympathetically.

Mr. Simons, who taught math and computers, enjoyed challenging his classes. His favorite method was to offer problems he hoped would stump the class and get them thinking. The boys were anything but enthused about the challenges Mr. Simons offered, but they continued nonetheless.

"Don't forget your math book this time," Mordechai warned Shmully. The three boys collected their things from their classroom and followed Dovid and Shimmy to the math and computer room.

Dovid and Shimmy were a rather mischievous pair. The stunts that they pulled often managed to keep things quite lively at school.

The boys arrived at their destination. The only other person there was Big Baruch. He had his feet up on his desk and was munching away on a package of crackers. Mr. Simons was nowhere to be seen.

"Maybe he's sick today," Mordechai said half-jokingly.

"No such luck," replied Dovid. "I saw him before lunch, hunched over one of the computers. I'm sure he'll be here any minute."

A few of the boys groaned.

"Can't someone do something about these math problems Mr. Simons keeps dishing out?" asked Shmully in a despairing tone. "Isn't there someone who can ask him to stop? I mean, what does he think, that we're computers or something?"

"Calm down, Shmully," Dovid said.

"Yeah," added Shimmy, exchanging a glance with Dovid. "And don't worry about class so much. You just never know what could happen."

The boys' conversation came to an abrupt end as Mr. Simons arrived, looking very pleased with himself. He stood for a moment in the doorway, surveying the room and rubbing his hands together in eager anticipation of the hour to come. Then he strode to the front of the room.

"Now, boys," he announced in his slightly nasal voice, "let's get started. We haven't a moment to lose. You should all appreciate the fact that I came in early to key today's problem into our math program and save you boys valuable time!"

Mr. Simons' face positively glowed as he watched the class take their places around the computer stations.

"Power up, boys!" he commanded, his voice crackling with excitement.

He watched as the boys pressed the power buttons on their computers and smiled as the room began to hum.

"Okay, fellas, now type the following command to bring up the math program and let the fun . . ."

"Uh, Mr. Simons," Shmully interrupted, waving his hand to get his teacher's attention.

"No interruptions now, Shmully," Mr. Simons replied with annoyance. "Wait until we're all started. How is it that you always seem to have some kind of question before we've even begun?"

"But Mr. Simons, my computer . . ."

"I said, don't interrupt!" said Mr. Simons angrily. "Now once again, to get into today's program, just type in . . . "

"They're not working!" said several different voices at once.

"What?" exploded Mr. Simons, striding over to the nearest computer. "Didn't I tell you to turn it on? What's with you boys today, anyway?"

Mr. Simons reached over to switch on the computer, whose screen was blank, but the switch was already in the on position and the power indicator button glowed green. He glanced over at the computer next to it. The screen of that computer also showed nothing, although the power seemed to be on. After quickly surveying the room, Mr. Simons realized that the problem was universal.

"What is going on here?" he demanded. No answer was forthcoming from the boys, who were secretly delighted with the interruption.

Mr. Simons bent over one of the keyboards. He punched a few buttons, turned the power on and off, all to no avail. He examined several other computers. Everything appeared to be in order except that the screens were all blank.

He stooped down and crawled under the computer table so he could examine the computers from behind. The boys tried their best not to laugh as they watched their teacher disappear on his hands and knees.

"Do you think someone rigged the computers?" Mordechai whispered to Dovid, who was seated next to him.

"Who knows?" replied Dovid, a twinkle in his eyes. "But whoever thought of it sure was brilliant, wouldn't you say?"

Their whispered conversation was cut short when the computer table they were seated at suddenly jolted upwards. This was accompanied by the sound of a loud exclamation.

"Ouch!" shouted Mr. Simons, reappearing a moment later and rubbing his head where he had bumped it under the computer table. "Some trick," he growled. "Now which of you fellows is the perpetrator of this foul deed? I expect whoever it is to hand over the missing monitor cords. Now!"

He glared at each of the boys in turn, standing with his arms crossed and tapping his foot.

"I don't know what he's after," Shmully muttered to Shimmy, "but I've got to go to the bathroom."

Shimmy just grinned as Shmully pushed back his chair and headed out the door.

"Excuse me, sir!" Mr. Simons' voice halted him in the doorway. "Where do you think you're off to at this most crucial moment?"

"To the bathroom, Mr. Simons," Shmully answered in a shaky voice. He quickly backed out the door and disappeared down the hall.

"Where are all the monitor cords?" Mr. Simons repeated threateningly. "I want them returned now, or the culprit will be in big trouble when he's discovered."

The threat was met with silence. For what seemed like an eternity, the boys sat quietly in front of their computers, hardly daring to move.

Suddenly, Shmully returned to the room, a cord dangling from his hands.

Mr. Simons whirled to face him. "Where did you get that?" he roared.

Shmully shook with fear and dropped the cord. Mr. Simons ran over and picked it up.

"Where are the rest?" Mr. Simons demanded of Shmully.

"The rest of what?" Shmully stuttered a reply.

"The monitor cords, that's what."

"Oh, is that what this is?" asked Shmully, his eyes wide. "I found it in the bathroom. I brought it back in case it was what you were looking for. There weren't any more." Shmully quickly found his seat.

"Hey, I think I remember seeing one of those by the washing stations in the lunchroom," chimed in another boy.

Mr. Simons surveyed the room with a furious glare. "Get out of here now, and find me the rest of the monitor cords," he shouted. "You all have five minutes!"

"This is as much fun as any scavenger hunt," Mordechai said as he and Levi went down the hall, knocking on each classroom door in search of the missing monitor cords.

"It sure beats doing one of Mr. Simons' math problems," Levi agreed. "I wonder who did it?"

"Well, it would have to have been someone who missed lunch, since Mr. Simons was setting up all the computers right before lunch and we were there right after," Mordechai said thoughtfully.

"Say, where were you during lunch, anyway?"

"I can't tell you, Mordechai. Sorry, but I promised."

"Well, I just hope Mr. Simons doesn't find out that you were missing," said Mordechai in a sulky voice, annoyed with Levi for holding out on him. "I'd hate to see what he'd do to you if he thought you were responsible."

"How's he ever going to find that out?" Levi asked nervously.

Mordechai just shrugged.

Fifteen minutes later, the two returned empty-handed to the classroom, where a still fuming Mr. Simons was trying to reattach a monitor cord.

"A screwdriver," he mumbled. "I need a screwdriver. You can't get these cords on or off without one."

He looked up and saw Mordechai and Levi standing in the doorway.

"Don't just stand there! Go to the janitor and get me a screwdriver!"

They dashed back out and down the hall, passing Shimmy and Dovid standing next to the drinking fountain.

"Where are you off to in such a rush?" Shimmy asked.

"Mr. Simons needs a screwdriver to reattach the cords he's collected so far," Mordechai replied.

"Well, don't rush, you know," Dovid warned. "There's still thirty minutes left of class time."

"That's true," replied Mordechai, and he and Levi continued down the hall at a much slower pace.

They passed the fountain again a few minutes later, returning with a screwdriver in hand. Dovid and Shimmy hadn't budged.

"Aren't you helping look for the cords?" Levi inquired curiously. "It's kind of fun, right?"

"What for?" Dovid asked. "The rest of the class seems to be doing a good enough job of it. Besides, we don't want them all found too soon."

"Mr. Simons might decide to have class after all if there's too much time left," Shimmy agreed.

"Well, see you later," Levi said with a wave. He and Mordechai turned into the classroom to give Mr. Simons the screwdriver.

Presently, Mr. Simons had reattached all the available cords. Though some of the cords were still missing, he demanded that all of the boys be rounded up for the last ten minutes of class. Quickly, the class was seated once again.

"Now, boys," said Mr. Simons in a deliberately controlled voice, "being that someone has managed to waste almost our entire math period, I have one small assignment for you to do right now."

The boys exchanged wary glances.

"I want you each to take out a piece of paper, and we'll play a little memory game."

He waited until each boy had a piece of paper

in front of him, then continued. "I want you to write down the name of the boy who sat on your right during lunch, then your own name, and then the name of the boy who sat on your left. Let's see if you can all remember that far back."

Mr. Simons' stern voice gave Levi chills as he realized, with a shock, what his teacher was after. Mr. Simons knew the boys wouldn't tell him outright who had been missing from the lunch room. He was attempting to trick them into providing him with the answer.

Levi was at a loss. He knew that if a paper wasn't passed in with his name on it, he would be in trouble. The only thing he could think of was to put down Baruch's name next to his. But who else should he put down? And what if Baruch didn't think to write down his name?

As Levi stared down at his paper, he heard Mordechai's voice.

"I'll collect these for you, Mr. Simons," Mordechai said, jumping up and starting to gather the completed papers.

Mordechai stopped at Levi's desk and snatched his paper. Now I'm really sunk, he thought. But Mordechai quickly crumpled the sheet he had collected from Levi and stuffed it in his pocket before he reached the next boy's seat.

What is Mordechai up to? Levi wondered.

He noticed that Baruch hadn't even attempted to write down any names. When Mordechai stopped by him, he simply shrugged his shoulders and didn't pass in a paper.

Mr. Simons snatched up the papers that Mordechai brought him and began to lay them out on his desk in the order of the seating arrangement that the boys had written. Levi looked on, growing more nervous with each paper laid down.

Suddenly, Dovid elbowed him to get his attention. He passed Levi a piece of paper folded the way Mordechai always folded his notes. Mr. Simons was too busy arranging the papers on his desk to notice Levi. Levi unfolded the note and read:

"Don't worry. I threw your paper out and passed in one for you. Since I was seated at the end of the bench, I just put you next to me on your paper and my own."

What a great friend Mordechai is, thought Levi. Then a small pang of worry hit him. "But what about Baruch?" he mouthed silently to Mordechai.

Mordechai just shrugged his shoulders. "Who cares?" he mouthed back.

He was right, of course, Levi told himself uneasily. Who did care about a bully like Big Baruch, anyway?

Mr. Simons arranged the papers in a neat stack. It seemed he had found his culprit.

"Aha," he said in a triumphant voice. "As I suspected. Baruch, I expect an explanation of where you were during this past lunch period. You certainly weren't in the lunch room, were you?"

Baruch scowled down at his desk. He wasn't about to announce to the whole class where he had been. Splitting one's pants was not something one wanted to publicize.

"I asked for an explanation, young man," Mr. Simons insisted, walking over to Baruch's side with long, purposeful strides.

Baruch kept his eyes glued downwards and doodled on a piece of paper.

Suddenly, Levi felt something burst inside him. He couldn't bear the injustice of the situation, even if Big Baruch was the victim.

"He was with me, Mr. Simons," Levi blurted out.

Mr. Simons spun around to face Levi.

"With you? With you? So, Mr. Newman, where were you during lunch time?"

"I really can't say," Levi mumbled, suddenly sorry that he had spoken.

"Maybe you two boys would rather explain this to the principal," he declared, beckoning to them both to follow.

He looked down at the sheets of paper in his hand. Something was bothering him.

"But I'm sure I saw your name somewhere," he said to Levi. He shuffled through the papers he held, looking for Levi's name.

"Wait . . . here it is. Just as I thought," he muttered, a few sheets fluttering down to the floor.

Shimmy bent over automatically to pick the

papers up for him. As he leaned over, a screwdriver fell out of his pocket with a loud clatter.

Mr. Simons looked up sharply from the papers he was studying. The screwdriver had fallen right at his feet. Slowly, he bent down to retrieve it from the floor.

"I believe this is yours, Shimmy," Mr. Simons said with a tight smile, making no move to return the incriminating tool. "Or perhaps it is yours, Dovid? Your name seems to be taped on it. Would you boys care to explain why you need a screwdriver in math class?"

Dovid held out his hand for it.

"Thanks for returning the screwdriver you borrowed last week, Shimmy . . ." Dovid began, but he was silenced by a withering glare from Mr. Simons.

The bell rang, a moment too late for Shimmy and Dovid. "Shimmy and Dovid, you will both follow me to the principal's office," said Mr. Simons firmly. "Levi and Baruch, looks like you're off the hook," he added. He gripped Shimmy's and Dovid's arms and led them away.

The rest of the boys quickly gathered up their things and left the room. Everyone was quite astonished at the rapid turn of events.

Mordechai fell in step next to Levi. "Wow, you sure lucked out," he exclaimed.

"I guess so," said a still stunned Levi.

"So, where were you during lunch, anyway?"

Shmully asked, coming up behind the pair.

Levi still didn't want to answer that question. He'd had enough trouble with Big Baruch already and wasn't looking for any more involvement with him. His hope quickly vanished, however.

"Hey, Newman!" called out an all too familiar voice as Levi, Mordechai and Shmully rounded the corner.

All three stopped suddenly and stared at Big Baruch, who was leaning against the wall with his arms crossed.

"Looks like trouble again," Mordechai whispered sharply to Levi. "And after what you just did for him, too."

Baruch beckoned to Levi.

"Uh, see ya later," Shmully said hastily. "I gotta go to the bathroom or get a drink or something." He swiftly disappeared down the hall.

Levi went over to Baruch while Mordechai waited nearby.

"I just wanted to say thanks, Newman," Baruch said. "Now I owe you double. I don't forget things, either, you know."

"Yeah, I know," Levi said. "But this time, do forget it, Baruch. It was nothing." And with that, he continued swiftly down the hall.

The bell rang for the next class. Mordechai caught up with Levi and jabbed him playfully in the side.

"Come on. We don't want to be late."

"I'm right behind you," Levi called. He hurried down the hall with Mordechai, temporarily pushing his conversation with Big Baruch out of his mind.

5

LEVI ARRIVED AT SCHOOL THE NEXT DAY ONLY TO have a swarm of boys surround him before he could even enter the school grounds.

"Levi the Tailor!" they chuckled as he headed for the building.

"Why didn't you let us know?" others mocked.

"What are you talking about?" Levi asked, trying to slip past the crowd of boys and up the school steps.

"Like he doesn't know or something!" said a laughing voice behind him as he finally managed to enter the building.

Inside it was no better. A new crowd surrounded Levi with the same chant.

"Levi the Tailor," they all laughed. "Levi the Tailor!"

Someone waved a paper in his face. He grabbed at it, and the big letters seemed to jump out at him:

```
┌────────────────────────────────────────┐
│          TAILORING BY LEVI             │
│           No job too small!            │
│   Mending . . . Sewing . . . Tailoring . . . │
│        Fast and efficient service      │
│          Competitive rates!            │
└────────────────────────────────────────┘
```

Written on the bottom was Levi's phone number.

Levi was speechless. He pushed his way through the throng of boys towards his locker. Each locker he passed had a copy of the leaflet stuck into its door. It was even posted on the bulletin board, where a large group of boys stood and read the advertisement.

"Levi the Tailor!" they laughed.

"Look, there he goes now!"

"Levi the Tailor, could you please fix my jacket. The pocket has holes."

"My zipper's broken," called out another. "How much will you charge?"

"Can I make an appointment for you to go over my wardrobe after school and give me some expert tailoring advice?" someone else pleaded mockingly, sending the crowd into new fits of laughter.

"Bug off, fellas," Levi said miserably. He ducked into his classroom as quickly as he could. Mercifully, the lesson started soon, sparing Levi any further taunting.

"Does anyone have an answer for me?" Reb Hirsh inquired of the class, breaking into Levi's troubled thoughts.

"I think that Levi the Tailor might be able to get it all sewed up for us," Dovid said loudly. The room broke into peals of laughter.

Reb Hirsh looked sternly at Dovid. "Did you say you would like to volunteer the answer to the class?" he chastised. Dovid merely shook his head.

Shimmy got up to sharpen his pencil. He left a note on Levi's desk as he passed.

"Your flyer really left me in stitches," it stated. Levi wasn't amused.

Another note soon followed. "I need a new suit for a *bar-mitzvah*. How soon can you get it done?"

Levi crumpled the note angrily.

The next note was from Mordechai. Levi knew that by the special way the note was folded.

"What's the bright idea, anyway? 'Levi the Tailor???' You've got to be kidding!"

Levi quickly wrote his reply and passed it back to Mordechai.

"I sure didn't do it. What kind of a fool do you

think I am, anyway? It must have been someone from the team who thinks I know how to sew."

Even to his best friend Mordechai, Levi had never confirmed the suspicion that he had learned how to sew.

When it was time for recess, Levi watched his classmates leave the room. He didn't have the heart to follow. He was quite aware of what awaited him if he did go.

Reb Hirsh looked up from his desk to see Levi sitting sadly in his seat. "What's all this about, Levi?" he asked quietly. He held up a copy of the flyer that one of the boys had left on his desk on the way out.

"I wish I knew," Levi replied.

"It's not your handiwork?" Reb Hirsh inquired.

"No," said Levi. "I would never advertise myself as Levi the Tailor. Look where it's gotten me so far. I haven't been left alone all morning. I can't even go out to recess."

"Well, you're going to have to face the boys sooner or later," Reb Hirsh replied thoughtfully. "It's probably better sooner than later. If you didn't make these flyers, why don't you just tell them so?"

"Because they'll never believe me, not in a million years. They're having too much fun teasing me. I'll have to come up with a better story."

"You know, sometimes the best story is the truth. Try telling the boys the truth and see what happens. You can't hide in here forever."

"I guess not," said Levi. "And I suppose at this point, I don't have that much to lose, anyway. Thanks, Reb Hirsh."

Slowly, Levi made his way down the hall, heading for the playground. He was spotted before he made it outside.

"Look, it's Levi the Tailor going out to solicit more business!" someone called out.

"Good," someone else added. "I just noticed a hole in my backpack. Please, Levi the Tailor, can you fix it?"

The hallway was soon full of teasing boys. Everyone was laughing except Levi.

"Look, guys," he said firmly, looking around at everyone. "I didn't put up those signs. I don't know anything about it. I'm certainly not a tailor, and I'm not interested in any business."

This speech only made the boys laugh even harder. "So who did it, if not you?" yelled someone from the back.

"I did," growled the unmistakable voice of Big Baruch. "You want to make something of it?"

The boys' laughter and jeers came to an abrupt end. The crowd simply melted away as soon as Big Baruch appeared beside Levi. Levi was left alone to face something that he couldn't help feeling might be worse than the taunting gang—a glaring Big Baruch.

"You don't like my signs, Newman?" he rumbled

as he backed Levi up against the wall. "I was just trying to repay what you did for me yesterday, but if you don't like it, then forget it."

His fist passed dangerously close to Levi's nose, but merely traveled upwards harmlessly to tear down the sign pinned on the bulletin board above Levi's head. Baruch spun on his heels and barreled down the hall, tearing down every "Levi the Tailor" sign he could find.

Levi ran outside to recess, where he nearly bumped into Mordechai, who was waiting by the door.

"You're okay?" Mordechai asked.

"Doing just great," Levi grumbled facetiously. "Wouldn't you be?"

"Well, at least you cleared things up with everyone," Mordechai said as they walked out together.

"I sure hope so," Levi replied. "I didn't realize that Big Baruch had done it."

"Well, who else did you think would do it? He's out to get you, remember? This was just his idea of a new way to lay a low blow on arch enemy number one . . . you."

"I don't think so, Mordechai," Levi said thoughtfully. "I mean after all, look how I got him out of trouble yesterday in Simons' class."

"Sure, Levi, but I don't think what you did makes all that much difference to a guy like Big Baruch. He just proved it to us today."

"But I don't think he intended this to be taken the way it was," Levi retorted. "I think he meant well."

"Right, Levi," said Mordechai in a sarcastic tone. "Look, if there ever was anyone who it isn't worth being *dan lekaf zchus*, it's a character like Big Baruch. So don't bother. Let's go see what they're up to in the game."

Mordechai broke into a sprint and headed for the ballfield, with Levi close at his heels.

"Hey, it's Levi the Tailor," called out Dovid when he caught sight of the pair.

"Cut it out, Dovid," called out Shimmy. "We know now that it was a set-up. Big Baruch's out to get him, and he almost had us all taken in, too."

"Yeah. What a low blow," Dovid agreed with disgust.

Later, as the boys returned to the school building, Levi turned to Mordechai and Shmully. "Maybe I shouldn't have gotten myself out of that mess," he said doubtfully. "It only got someone else into trouble."

"Better him than you," Mordechai declared. "Besides, he got himself into trouble. No one asked him to tell the world that he made the flyers."

"True," Levi agreed thoughtfully. "But I still feel bad."

"After all he planned to do to you?" asked a surprised Shmully. "I sure wouldn't worry about a guy like that."

Levi wasn't satisfied. "He doesn't deserve the kind of treatment all the guys are dishing out. He's still a person, isn't he?" he asked.

Mordechai and Shmully exchanged confused glances.

"Don't worry about it so much, okay?" Mordechai concluded as they entered the classroom. But Levi continued to worry.

Sleep didn't come easily that night for Levi. The dark shadows under his eyes proved it in the morning.

"You look sick, Levi," said Perel, his five-year-old sister, in a matter-of-fact tone. Mrs. Newman looked Levi over as Perel turned her attention back to her bowl of Cheerios.

Seven-year-old Brachah, taking advantage of her sister's preoccupation, quickly moved the cereal to her own side of the table and immersed herself in reading the back of the box. A few spoonfuls later, Perel noticed that the cereal box was missing and let out a cry of protest when she saw her sister hiding behind it.

Mrs. Newman, having studied Levi and quickly assessed what appeared a simple case of sleep deprivation, discarded Perel's observation of Levi's condition and turned her attention to the girls.

But unlike the momentary childish spat, which was quickly solved, Levi's problem stayed on his mind throughout the day.

6

Levi's PARENTS EXCHANGED GLANCES AT THE dinner table. They were both concerned about their unusually quiet son. The sharp contrast between Levi's silence and the characteristic tumult generated by the rest of the family was an obvious sign to them that something was amiss.

The other children took no notice of Levi. In fact, Levi's silence just made it easier for each of them to be heard when placing their food orders, which they did habitually, although their mother already knew what each of her children required at mealtime.

For Perel, it was plenty of meat loaf and mixed vegetables except for the carrots. Brachah would rather forego the meat loaf, but enjoyed mixed vegetables and mashed sweet potatoes. She was served the meat loaf anyway. Yehudis, the baby, ate whatever she wasn't busy throwing over her high chair tray. Chaim, the three-year-old, simply refused any supper at all until he was bribed with the crunchy corners of the meat loaf and allowed to pick all of the lima beans out of his vegetables.

Levi, like his siblings, usually had his own particular food preferences. Tonight, however, he simply ate whatever he was served mechanically and didn't contribute to the dinner conversation. He was lost in thought, trying to decide if he was responsible for what had happened to Big Baruch.

Both parents felt it would be best to let Levi work out whatever was bothering him by himself. They were confident Levi knew that if he needed them, they were there.

"I'm going into the study to prepare for my shiur," Mr. Newman excused himself after bentching.

Levi glanced at his watch and noted that it would be time for his father to leave for his nightly shiur in less than an hour. He decided to try to speak to him before then.

He poked his head into the study where Mr. Newman sat at his desk bent over a sefer. Levi decided he couldn't bother his father when he was involved in his learning. Maybe he'd try again later.

However, Mr. Newman had been listening carefully just in case Levi decided to discuss whatever it was that was troubling him. He heard the squeak of Levi's sneakers as he turned to go.

"Levi, come in," he called out, closing his *sefer*. "What can I do for you?"

Levi looked down at the floor, absent-mindedly tracing a pattern in the carpet with the toe of his sneaker. He wasn't quite sure where to begin. Should he start with the favors he had done for Big Baruch and the way he was paid back, the terrible day when he was tormented by Big Baruch's bullying, or perhaps even the very beginning, the uniform incident? He decided on the second choice.

"Well, I think this all started when I offered to take care of sewing the team emblems on our new baseball uniforms," Levi began.

Mr. Newman listened closely while Levi proceeded to tell him the whole story.

"I just feel awful now whenever I think about it," concluded Levi after tracing events up to the present. "I mean, is it right for me to be so worried about myself, if it just means that someone else will be hurt instead, even if that someone is the school's biggest bully? Am I responsible for everyone blaming Baruch and thinking that he's still bullying me?"

Mr. Newman, who had expected that Levi's

problem would be the bullying itself, was surprised to find that Levi's real concern was the hurt feelings Big Baruch might be suffering. He looked at his son fondly, proud of the consideration that he displayed for others, but uncertain of what to advise him. He sat pondering the question for several minutes. Finally, the silence was broken as Mr. Newman cleared his throat.

"Levi, your question of whether you are responsible for things said afterwards about this fellow seems to be simple enough to answer."

Levi leaned forward in his seat.

"I don't believe that what happened was your fault. You couldn't possibly have known who had written the flyers, that he would admit it or what the consenquences might be."

Levi heaved a sigh of relief, but his father was not yet finished. "It is my opinion, though, that since you have shown such sensitivity to this whole issue, it can't possibly hurt, and would probably do a tremendous amount of good, if you tried to right some of the wrong that was done."

"What do you mean?" asked Levi.

"I think that you should try to make things up to this boy. Attempt some friendly overtures. The other boys believe this fellow was out to get you. If you, of all people, are friendly to him, the basis for all those rumors will just fall away."

"But you just said it wasn't my fault!" cried Levi.

"Yes, you're right. It really wasn't your fault, but since this whole incident still troubles you so much, why not attempt to make things better?"

"Great idea, Tatti, except for one thing," Levi replied. "You seem to have forgotten who we're talking about here. We're talking about the biggest bully in the school. No one goes near him if he can help it. I told you what he did to me before. What do you think is going to happen to me now if I go anywhere near him? I can't see that there's any chance of him being anyone's friend, especially not mine." Levi sighed resignedly.

Mr. Newman looked at Levi pointedly. "You've never given him the chance, Levi. It doesn't sound like anyone has. Just try it. You're always having friends spend *Shabbos* here. Why don't you invite him for *Shabbos* sometime? You can decide then if being his friend is really as impossible as you make it out to be. I think you'll find that it's worth the attempt. I think you'll find there's more to this bully than meets the eye.

"It's in your hands to change things," Mr. Newman concluded. "Don't give up without even trying."

He glanced over at the clock and stood up. It was time for him to leave for his *shiur*. He gave Levi's shoulder a reassuring squeeze.

"I know you have it in you, Levi. Think it over." He put on his jacket and hat and picked up his *Gemara*.

"Learn well," Levi called after his father's departing figure.

Levi sat pondering a while in the quiet of the study. It could be that Tatti has a point, he thought. Maybe Big Baruch never has been given a chance. But who in his right mind would try to become friends with such a person, let alone spend an entire *Shabbos* with him? Tatti just doesn't seem to understand exactly who Big Baruch is, Levi concluded.

No, Levi decided, I'm just not interested in having anything more to do with Big Baruch. If Tatti feels that I'm not to blame for what occurred, then I'll leave it at that. To do more would just be asking for trouble.

"I TOLD YOU I DON'T FORGET THINGS," SAID BIG
Baruch to Levi, whom he had cornered on the way
to school the next morning. "I don't want you to
forget, either, how great things were going before
you managed to spread all those rumors about
me. Maybe when I'm finished with you, you'll
know what real *hakaros hatov* is. You'll appreciate
how your life used to be before you started fooling
around with Big Baruch!"

Levi knew he was in for it now. In his wildest
dreams, he had never imagined that Big Baruch
would blame him for starting the rumors.

"It wasn't me Baruch, really!" he begged, but the look in Big Baruch's eyes was anything but sympathetic.

"I don't like guys trying to step on a reputation I've managed to build up over the years," said Big Baruch, his voice heavy with sarcasm.

"Really, Baruch, I never said anything bad about you. You know me—I even stood up for you in Simons' class."

"Right," said Baruch. "That was only to save your own skin. You missed lunch too that day. Remember?"

"No," Levi argued. "I knew Mordechai put my name down on his lunch table list. It was only for your sake that I spoke up. I would have done the same for any of my friends, honest."

"Friend, huh? I've never been your friend, Newman, and don't start pretending it's any different now."

"How about if I proved to you that I thought of us as friends?" Levi asked suddenly. He knew he needed to choose his words carefully to avoid an outright lie.

"Sure, Newman, you go ahead and prove to me what good friends we are," said Big Baruch, standing with his arms crossed and an amused glint in his eyes.

"Just last night, I spoke with my father about inviting you for *Shabbos*. Now if that doesn't say something, what else does?"

"You expect me to believe that?"

"Would I lie to you?" Levi asked, in what he hoped was his most convincing tone.

"Maybe," replied Baruch, "if it came to wriggling out of a mess that you've managed to get yourself into. I'll tell you what—I'll call your bluff. I accept your kind invitation. I'll be there for *Shabbos*. I wouldn't want to refuse such a good friend, now would I?"

With that, Big Baruch dusted off his hands dramatically, picked up his backpack and strolled off towards school, leaving Levi to wonder what he had gotten himself into.

Later that day, with the morning encounter with Big Baruch behind him and lunch just ahead, Levi slipped into a seat in the lunchroom next to Mordechai. Mordechai had asked his close friends to meet at a table during lunch. Mordechai was already there, reserving their seats and waiting expectantly for the rest of the boys to show up.

When everyone had arrived, Mordechai began. "I want to invite you all to my house this *Shabbos*. My mom wants to put together a *shalosh seudos* for us. You know how it is when my mother throws something like this. It won't be just your regular *shalosh seudos*! You'll all be there, right?"

"You bet," Shmully said enthusiastically. "I wouldn't miss an invitation to your house for anything."

"We'll be there too," added Dovid, looking across

the table at Shimmy, who nodded in agreement.

Mordechai glanced over at Levi, who was trying to appear completely engrossed in his sandwich and potato chips. It was hard to ignore Mordechai, however, who elbowed Levi in the side, almost causing him to lose most of his chips.

"You'll be there too, right?" he asked suspiciously.

Levi took his time chewing and swallowing some potato chips. He did some quick thinking in the interim. Big Baruch was obviously not invited—not to mention that even if he was, he probably would have no interest in attending. Levi was also very reluctant to admit that Big Baruch would be at his house for *Shabbos*. He took a final swallow of his chips.

"I'm afraid not," he replied, avoiding Mordechai's eyes. "I'm going to be having some company, and I just don't think I'll be able to get away."

"That's no problem," said Mordechai generously. "Bring your company too!"

That was just about the last thing that Levi wanted to hear. He choked on a piece of potato chip and gave Mordechai a half-hearted smile of agreement. Mordechai thumped him vigorously on the back.

Just what Mordechai would love, Levi thought to himself grimly. Big Baruch there to create the right mood for all of his friends.

On his way home, Levi realized that there was

one thing left to do. He had to check with his mother to make sure that it would be okay for him to invite a friend for *Shabbos*. He didn't think that it would be a problem, since he often invited friends, and besides, today was only Tuesday. His mother couldn't have made any plans for *Shabbos* yet.

"Mom," began Levi while Mrs. Newman was putting supper in the oven, "I want to invite a friend for *Shabbos*."

"That's nice, dear. You know you're always free to invite your friends for *Shabbos*. It will have to be next week, though, because I just promised Brachah this morning that she could invite Rochel. You know it's only fair that she have a chance, and she's been after me for a few weeks now to let her invite her friend."

"It's kinda important, Mom," begged Levi. "Can't you let me have my friend too?"

"You know how I feel about that, Levi. Having a friend for *Shabbos*, especially at Brachah's age, is a special experience for both her and her friend. I don't want to take away any attention that she and her guest deserve by overdoing it with company. Next week is just another seven days away. Then your guest will get the same special attention."

Levi knew there was no point in arguing. His mother was very set in her ways on some issues, and this seemed to be one of them. But he still had a chance. If Brachah had only spoken to their mother this morning, maybe she hadn't asked her friend yet.

He ran up the steps and into Brachah's room. Perel, Chaim and Yehudis were also there.

"Brachah!" Levi called, out of breath.

Brachah, engrossed in her play, didn't bother turning around. Her hair was hidden under a *tichel*. Her feet made loud clumping noises in a pair of her mother's old high heels.

"There's no Brachah in this room," Perel informed him. "We're at a *chasunah*. Were you invited too?"

Perel was dressed the same way as her sister, but in addition to the *tichel* on her head, she had wrapped one around her waist as a fancy skirt.

Levi had no time for games. This was too important. "Come on, Brachah. I need to ask you something!" he insisted.

"That's Mrs. Cohen," Chaim chimed in. "Brachah couldn't come to this *chasunah*. She wasn't invited."

Chaim, who was wearing one of his father's old ties, was trying to help Yehudis tie on a *tichel*. Her feet were already inside a pair of Brachah's shoes.

Any other time, Levi might have been amused by the play-acting, but at this moment, he was only irritated.

"Okay," he began again. "Mrs. Cohen, I must speak to you."

Brachah looked up at Levi. "Can I help you, sir?" she inquired coolly. "I must be on my way to this *chasunah*, you know. My neighbor's daughter is getting married."

"I don't care who's getting married. I need to know if you already invited your friend Rochel for *Shabbos*."

"Rochel? Rochel, you ask? I don't know any Rochel. I do have a friend named Mrs. Bernstein, though. She comes to my house every *Shabbos*. Would you like to come too?"

Levi was growing more annoyed by the moment. "Look here, Brachah . . . Mrs. Cohen, I mean. Just answer me, okay? Then I'll go away and leave you alone."

"Sure, I invited her," replied Brachah, dropping her character for a moment. "Mommy said she'd buy us cookies with sprinkles for a *Shabbos* party. I told Rochel, and she can't wait to come."

"Can't she come next week instead?" Levi asked with mounting desperation.

"No, because Mommy said she's buying the sprinkle cookies this week," Brachah replied logically.

"Well, just tell her to buy them next week."

"No, by next *Shabbos* Rochel's going to be at her Bubby and Zeidy's in Florida, where she's going for two weeks. That's why she has to come this week."

Levi knew he had lost and left his siblings to

continue their game. Now what am I going to do, he thought? Tell Big Baruch that he can't come after all? Somehow, I don't think Big Baruch will accept any excuses. He'll probably just finish where he left off in giving me that lesson in "*hakaros hatov.*"

Levi was usually not given to procrastination, but this was one time he simply couldn't bring himself to do what he had to. Wednesday and Thursday passed without him being able to summon up the courage to speak to Big Baruch.

Thursday night at dinner, Levi tried to block out thoughts about what tomorrow would most certainly bring.

"Please pass the ketchup," Chaim called out. "Please pass the ketchup! Please . . ."

"Chaim," Mrs. Newman said. "How many times have I told you, please specify which person you are addressing. Otherwise, no one pays you a bit of attention."

"Okay, then please pass the ketchup, Mommy," said Chaim, grinning.

Mrs. Newman looked momentarily surprised. She hadn't been aware that the ketchup was right next to her the whole time.

"Oh, Mommy," Brachah said. "I forgot to tell you that . . ."

"What, dear?" Mrs. Newman asked with mild interest.

"Rochel can't come. They're leaving early for

Florida. They want to spend an extra *Shabbos* there this week. Rochel also said that her Bubby's going to buy her sprinkle cookies there too, and not just for *Shabbos!*"

"That's nice for her, Brachah. You'll have to remember to invite her again when she gets back."

Levi couldn't believe his ears. He felt a tremendous load had just been lifted off his mind.

"I'll buy you sprinkle cookies too," he told Brachah gratefully. "One for every day that Rochel is gone."

Brachah looked up at him in surprise.

"Why?" she asked.

"For saving my life," Levi answered fervently.

"Me too?" Perel asked.

"And me," added Chaim.

"Cookie!" said Yehudis, pushing away her half-eaten supper.

"What's all this about, Levi?" Mrs. Newman asked.

"Well, since we were planning on having a guest anyway, do you suppose I could have my friend after all, now that Rochel's not coming?"

"Well, it is quite late to first invite someone, don't you think?" she replied doubtfully.

"I'm sure he won't mind, Mom. Please, why don't you let me just see if it's okay with him?"

"Fine, Levi. You can call him up first thing after dinner, and then let me know."

"He'll come, Mom. I guarantee it."

8

SHABBOS WAS STARTING IN THIRTY MINUTES. LEVI kept finding himself checking his watch and any other clock he could find. Big Baruch hadn't arrived yet.

I'll believe it when I see it, Levi said to himself as he headed down the stairs on a last-minute errand for his mother. Suddenly, he stopped dead in his tracks. Was that a knock on the door? He jumped down the rest of the steps two at a time and paused in front of the door before opening it.

How could I have gotten myself into spending an entire *Shabbos* with Baruch? Levi wondered.

Another, more persistent, knock on the door brought Levi back to the present. He pulled open the door, and there stood Baruch. Or at least the hulking figure *seemed* to be Baruch. It was difficult to tell exactly who was behind the tremendous bouquet of flowers the visitor was holding.

"My mother sent these for your mother," said Baruch with obvious distaste, thrusting the bouquet into a surprised Levi's hands.

The two boys stood eying each other for a few moments until Levi remembered his manners.

"Come in, please," he said cordially. "I'm glad you made it."

An instant later, Brachah, Perel, and Chaim came racing over to see who was at the door. They were thrilled to see the *Shabbos* guest and promptly took him into the family room where they kept all of their toys.

Chaim led the way, tugging on his new friend's hand and discussing his favorite dump truck.

"It's yellow and very big," he prattled. "You can play with it this *Shabbos* if you want."

Perel, not to be outdone, danced alongside the boys trying to get Baruch's attention.

"We've got lots of *mentchies* to play with," she said, indicating the children's collection of *Fisher Price* figures. "If you want, when we divide them up, we can make a pile for you. You can always trade if you don't like the ones you get."

Brachah had her own comments to add.

"Mommy made lots of special stuff just because we have a *Shabbos* guest. She even bought some cookies with sprinkles for a *Shabbos* party. Do you like sprinkle cookies? Rochel does, but she couldn't come."

"Let me take care of these flowers," Levi said to Baruch, trying to make himself heard over the ruckus. "I guess these guys will keep you busy! I'll just take your bag upstairs and finish up something for my mother. I'll be right back."

Moments later, Levi returned to the family room and stopped short in astonishment.

"Giddy-up, horsie!" Chaim called out enthusiastically, digging his heels into the sides of his mount, who was none other than Big Baruch.

"Giy-up!" added Yehudis. She clutched Chaim's waist while Perel held her in place on Baruch's back.

"Whoa, boy," Brachah said. She patted Baruch's head and pulled on the jump rope with which she was leading him.

"I'm back," Levi finally managed to mumble, though no one in the room gave him so much as a glance. He sat down on the couch to watch the spectacle.

Minutes later, Mr. Newman called Levi and Baruch to leave for *shul*. Baruch carefully unloaded his passengers and disentangled himself from the jump rope.

"Where are you going?" Perel inquired.

"To *shul*," Baruch replied as he tucked in his shirt.

"Can't you just stay home with us?" Chaim pleaded.

"Sorry," said Baruch. "I'll see you guys later. Good *Shabbos*."

Levi followed Baruch out of the room and into the front hall where Mr. Newman was waiting. "Ready?" asked Mr. Newman.

Both of the boys nodded.

"Then we're off. Good *Shabbos*!" Mr. Newman called out.

"Good *Shabbos*! Good *Shabbos*!" all the children called as they ran to the window to wave good bye to their father, Levi and especially Baruch.

"How many brothers and sisters do you have?" Levi asked conversationally on the way home from *shul*, sure that this would be a good way to get Baruch talking. We might even have siblings who are the same age, Levi thought.

But plans of a smooth conversation with Big Baruch ended with his abrupt reply, "None." The two boys walked the rest of the way home in silence.

When they returned home, Levi couldn't help but notice that his siblings all seemed to be in the exact same place he had left them, standing at the window waving frantically. It was as if they had been waiting for Baruch all that time.

"Good *Shabbos*," Mr. Newman said, entering the house and swinging Yehudis up into his arms.

"Good *Shabbos!*" Brachah, Perel, and Chaim called out enthusiastically, aiming their greeting at one person in particular, Baruch.

Brachah and Perel escorted Baruch to his seat at the table. "Tonight you sit next to me," explained Brachah.

"And tomorrow you'll be over here next to me," added Perel.

Chaim was already seated. The seat he occupied was, of course, Baruch's. Baruch seemed to read Chaim's mind — he simply picked him up, sat down in the chair and placed the little boy squarely on his lap.

Mr. Newman started to sing *Shalom Aleichem*. Baruch sang in an undertone that even Chaim couldn't hear.

Chaim wanted to make sure that Baruch knew the routine. "It's time for *Aishes Chaim* now," he declared. Chaim, as usual, insisted that *Aishes Chaim* was the proper beginning for the *zemer*.

Brachah passed a *bentcher* opened to the right page to Baruch. Baruch got the message, and his voice rang out clear and strong as he joined in the singing.

"Levi, you aren't singing *Aishes Chayil* with us," Perel whispered.

"You're right," said Levi with a start. "I was just listening to Baruch. I never knew he could sing, and I *daven* with him every day at school."

"Well, he won't know you can sing either if you don't start," Perel replied. Chastened, Levi joined in for the rest of the *zemer*.

Even if he had had a lot to say, Levi didn't have much chance to speak to Baruch at the meal. Baruch was the center of attention. He chatted good-naturedly with all of the children and even managed to successfully slip Chaim back on his own chair. Levi was somewhat relieved that his guest was kept occupied without him after his failed attempt at conversation on the way home from *shul*.

"Pass the food to Baruch," Mrs. Newman instructed, always afraid that a guest might still be hungry.

"Here, have some rice," Brachah said as she passed it to Baruch.

"He doesn't have any salad left," Perel pointed out.

"Do you think I could have some of that too?" Mr. Newman asked good-naturedly, indicating one of the numerous dishes which the children had placed next to Baruch's plate.

"So!" began Mrs. Newman. "You live just three blocks away, and we've never seen you around. Imagine! Of course, I have met your mother at various functions. Please be sure to thank her for the lovely bouquet."

Baruch barely had a chance to nod when he

found Chaim, who had already finished eating, quietly crawling back onto his lap.

"Chaim, come here," Levi ordered. "I'm done, so I'll hold you while Baruch finishes eating."

"That's okay," said Baruch. "I'm finished too."

"Brachah, Perel and Chaim, if you want to have dessert, first go put on your pajamas," announced Mrs. Newman.

Perel and Brachah ran upstairs to comply. Chaim didn't budge.

"Chaim, I said pajamas, or aren't you having dessert?"

"How come she doesn't have to put on her pajamas?" Chaim asked, pointing at Yehudis and pouting.

"She will. You can bring her pajamas on your way down."

With the younger children upstairs, the room seemed unusually silent. Levi noticed his mother look at him strangely, wondering why he and his friend seemed to have nothing to say to one another. He felt he had to break the silence somehow.

"I don't suppose you brought your *Mishnayos* with you?" he asked Baruch. "I've been spending the past few *Shabbosim* reviewing for the test. Maybe we can do that tomorrow afternoon, if we have a chance."

"Fine," Baruch replied.

Chaim, Perel and Brachah, now in pajamas,

came bounding down the stairs. Mrs. Newman disappeared into the kitchen to get dessert while Levi helped clear the table. Brachah wouldn't allow Baruch to lift a finger.

"You're the guest," she insisted. "You're just supposed to enjoy yourself. Right, Tatti?"

Mr. Newman nodded in agreement. "He's certainly exempt, especially if he joins me in the next round of *zemiros*."

From the kitchen, Levi listened to Baruch's voice harmonizing with his father's. Maybe this *Shabbos* won't be so bad after all, he thought to himself.

9

SHABBOS AFTERNOON FOUND LEVI AND BARUCH sitting at the dining room table, ready to begin their study session. "Where should we start?" Levi asked.

"Let's start at the beginning," Baruch replied.

Levi automatically assumed that he was doing Baruch a favor by learning with him. He wasn't sure how much real studying he'd accomplish this way. After all, Baruch rarely participated in class. To Levi, that seemed to be a clear sign that Baruch didn't have anything worth saying in class.

Levi took the lead and began the first *Mishnah*.

It had been a long time since they had done this one in class, and he was almost immediately stumped. Much to his surprise, Baruch took over where he left off. Baruch's voice was sure and strong. He seemed to be right in his element.

So why does it always look like he's not even listening in class? wondered Levi. I can't remember him ever participating.

Levi couldn't afford to let his thoughts continue to wander. He had to keep his mind on the *Mishnayos* if he wanted to have any chance of keeping up with Baruch.

It wasn't until almost two hours later that the two boys decided to call it quits. Levi now realized that Baruch would be a great *chavrusa* to help him prepare for the *Mishnayos* test. If only it wasn't Big Baruch the bully, thought Levi sadly.

As soon as Levi and Baruch stood up, scraping their chairs across the floor, Brachah, Perel, Chaim and Yehudis, who had been waiting at the door for them to finish, burst into the room.

"It's time for our *Shabbos* party," they chorused, leading the way into the kitchen, where Mrs. Newman had prepared a generous snack.

Baruch found himself with Chaim on one knee and Yehudis on the other, each of them happily munching away on whatever he put down on his plate.

"I told you we were going to have sprinkle cookies!" said Brachah happily as she passed

Baruch the plate of cookies.

"You forgot a *mezonos*," Perel told Baruch, after observing him eat his cookie without her having heard his *brachah*.

"Thanks, Perel. I made my *brachah* quietly," Baruch told her. When he drank his soda, he made sure to make the *brachah* loud enough for Perel to hear.

Perel went over to Levi and climbed onto his lap.

"I'll help you with your *brachos*, too," she said through a mouthful of corn chips as she reached for the last cookie, which happened to be on Levi's plate.

"Yeah, you're a big help all right," Levi said jokingly. "You're just making sure that I don't have anything to worry about making a *brachah* on."

Baruch looked at Levi. He glanced at Perel, who was still on Levi's lap, and offered his first friendly comment to Levi that *Shabbos*.

"You sure are lucky to have such a big family," he said quietly.

"Yeah, I guess so," Levi replied, never really having thought about it before.

He reached over to pull the bowl of corn chips away from Yehudis, just in the nick of time. In hot pursuit of the chips, she had pulled the bowl dangerously close to the edge of the table.

Levi gathered from Baruch's comment that it

must be hard for him to have no brothers or sisters, not to mention no friends. The least Levi could do was to try to improve the latter problem. He decided to take the first step now.

"Baruch," he said hesitantly. "Mordechai invited both of us to his house for *shalosh seudos*. He's going to be having lots of the guys in the neighborhood over. I'm sure you'll join me, right?"

Baruch glared at Levi, his customary scowl back on his face.

"No thanks," he replied presently and returned to bouncing Yehudis and Chaim on his knees. "You just go without me. It's not like your friends interest me, anyway."

Chaim, who had been following the exchange with a growing look of concern on his face, slipped off of Baruch's lap and trotted over to Levi.

"You're still gonna go, right?" he asked, tugging on his brother's shirt sleeve. "Mommy said that if you go, I'm also invited to play with Yehuda."

"I don't think I'll be going, Chaim," Levi said softly. He knew that good *midos* dictated he stay home with his guest, but he wasn't quite sure how to explain the concept to his little brother, especially in front of the very guest in question.

Chaim burst into tears. Not even an offer of the last piece of licorice at the table was enough to console him.

Baruch looked on for a few moments with feigned indifference as Levi tried to calm down the little boy. Then, much to Levi's surprise, Baruch's deep voice broke through Chaim's sobs.

"I'll go," he said.

Chaim's crying stopped instantly. He raised his tear-stained face and asked, "Does that mean that you're going too?"

"Yes," replied Levi with a smile. "All three of us are going."

Yehudis immediately left the room and reappeared a moment later dragging her coat.

"Go!" she demanded, struggling to put her arms in her coat sleeves.

Levi saw his other two sisters exchanging glances. He was sure it wouldn't be long before they'd also be crying in hopes of being granted the honor of accompanying the boys. To avoid more of a scene, Levi tickled Perel and Brachah and soon had them giggling. Yehudis joined in the fun, and was laughing so much she didn't even notice that Levi had extricated her from her coat.

"I'm going to get my shoes," Chaim announced. "Don't go without me."

He came back with both shoes on, though on the wrong feet. Levi put Chaim on his lap and quickly switched his shoes and tied them. Chaim got off and stood in front of Levi for inspection.

"I'm all ready to go," he said.

Levi took another look at him. "Chaim," he said, "where's your *yarmulka*?"

Chaim felt his bare head. "My head's not

tznius," he stated matter-of-factly, and he left to find his *yarmulka*.

Levi smiled and heard Baruch chuckle too.

"Girls, why don't you pick a book for me to read to you," Mrs. Newman called, trying to distract them so the boys could leave without the usual fuss that accompanied such departures.

Levi and Chaim slipped out with Baruch tip-tocing right behind. Levi quietly closed the front door. Unfortunately, Baruch was unaware of the screen door's habits. The boys' attempt to leave quietly was for naught, and they felt guilty when the door slammed behind them.

"Still think I'm lucky to have so many kids in the family?" Levi couldn't help but tease Baruch a little.

Baruch's only reply was a faint smile. This was the first personal thought that Levi had ever directed at Baruch, and he felt that his attempt was successful. Maybe we're actually making some progress, he thought.

Nevertheless, Levi was quite pleased with Chaim's company, since his constant chatter assured that there were none of the awkward silences that the two older boys had experienced earlier. Chaim held onto one of each of their hands.

As they neared Mordechai's house, Chaim released his grip on the boys' hands and ran ahead to be the first one at the door. He waited eagerly until both Levi and Baruch stood beside him before knocking. But impatient as ever, he followed that first knock with another louder one about three seconds later, feeling that ample time had been granted for a reply. The door swung open just as Chaim raised his fist for a third try.

"Good *Shabbos*, Chaim," greeted Mordechai. "Yehuda was hoping you would come."

"Good *Shabbos*!" Chaim called over his shoulder as he slipped past Mordechai. He had been there often enough to know just where to look for Yehuda and quickly disappeared.

"Good *Shabbos*, Levi," Mordechai greeted cordially. "Come in. All the other guys are here."

Baruch, who was standing near the doorway and shifting his weight uncomfortably, went unnoticed by Mordechai. He trailed Levi as they followed Mordechai into the dining room, where the others were already seated.

"Levi's here!" Shmully called out in greeting.

"Levi, come sit over here," called Dovid.

"This seat is better," Shimmy said. "It's right by the gourmet jelly beans."

"We can fix that," retorted Dovid, reaching across the table for the bowl of jelly beans.

Despite the commotion generated by the boys, Levi managed to spot two empty seats and headed for them. Baruch, following behind, hesitated in the doorway for a moment to take in his surroundings. As soon as his unmistakable bulk filled the doorway, a hush came over the room. Dovid sat back down in his chair, the bowl of jelly beans forgotten.

Baruch's face adopted its familiar scowl. Ignoring the cold reception, he headed for the seat next to Levi, seemingly oblivious to the stares of the boys around him.

"He's your guest?" Dovid inquired, the first to break the silence.

"Looks that way, doesn't it?" Levi replied briefly. He got up to wash, with Baruch following right behind.

When they returned, the other boys seemed to have recovered from their initial surprise and were again talking and laughing.

"So Baruch, what brings you to Levi's house?" Shimmy asked.

"I was invited," was the cold reply.

"Gosh, I never knew you guys were friends," Shmully began, but he turned bright red when he saw Big Baruch glare at him. "Uh, I mean it's really nice that you are getting along now after . . ." he stammered, finally deciding that it might be best to just keep quiet.

Mordechai also seemed more than a little taken aback by the situation. Levi kept looking up to find Mordechai staring at him in a rather cold and quizzical manner. As the afternoon wore on, Levi noticed that none of Mordechai's usual comments or jokes were directed towards him. He began to feel that he had fallen from his best friend's good graces.

Maybe I should have explained to Mordechai what was going on before I came, Levi thought. But it's obviously too late for that now.

Even though Mordechai made Levi feel awkward, he saw that his father had been right. The boys certainly couldn't point to Levi as Big Baruch's enemy now that it was known that they had spent *Shabbos* together. The rumors would stop, Levi hoped, although Mordechai's disapproval seemed a high cost to pay.

Levi soon forgot his worries over Mordechai as he became absorbed in the conversation around him. "Have you started working on the *Mishnayos* test yet?" Mordechai asked Shmully.

"Sure," came the reply. "I've been working on it every night. It's tough going."

"My father promised me he'd help," said Mordechai.

"Dovid and I are going to prepare together," Shimmy added.

"That's what I could use," Shmully said glumly, "a good *chavrusa*."

Levi stole a glance at Big Baruch sitting next to him. I've already found a good *chavrusa*, he thought to himself, so why not take advantage of it?

"Baruch," Levi said as the two boys walked home after *Maariv*, "do you think that maybe you would be interested in helping me prepare for the

Mishnayos test? Maybe we could learn together a couple nights a week."

Baruch stopped in his tracks and glared hard at Levi.

"Look, I don't need any more of your attempts at mock friendship, Newman," he retorted to the surprised Levi. "One *Shabbos* was enough for both of us to prove a point. As for the *Mishnayos* test, I'm sure you'll manage quite well on your own. Don't think I'm fool enough to think that my learning with you would be to your advantage!"

"That's not true, Baruch," Levi tried again. "I really do mean that you'd be helping me. You have no idea how much I gained from the couple of hours we spent learning together today. I'm not asking you to learn with me in order to be nice to you. I really could use the help. If you think it would just be a waste of time for you, then, of course, I wouldn't want you to do it."

After what seemed like an endless pause, Baruch slowly nodded his head.

"We'll give it a try," he said, "starting Monday after school."

Levi was thrilled. Suddenly, the *Mishnayos* test didn't seem all that scary any more. Nor, for that matter, did Big Baruch.

10

AT SUNDAY'S BALL PRACTICE, LEVI NOTICED THAT Mordechai seemed to be keeping his distance. Levi hoped that he was just imagining things. Just to make sure, he positioned himself next to Mordechai for the warm-up exercises Coach Friedman always put them through.

"Hey, Mordechai," he managed to whisper between push-ups, "the *shalosh seudos* was really great."

Mordechai just grunted in response, seemingly preoccupied with the all-important task at hand. To Levi, though, it felt like a deliberate snub.

This probably all stems from bringing Big Baruch with me to Mordechai's house on *Shabbos*, Levi thought. But after all, Mordechai had invited me to bring my guest along. He hadn't asked, or seemed to care, whom it might be. Yet now he's mad at me!

Mordechai confirmed Levi's suspicions later when the two boys waited for their turn at bat.

"I saw the way you and Big Baruch were acting yesterday," Mordechai said bitterly. "You two must really be good buddies now or something. Since when, anyway? I thought you and I were friends."

"Of course you and I are friends," Levi retorted, shocked by the hurt in his friend's voice. "Baruch and I are just learning together now. We're preparing for the *Mishnayos* test."

"Oh," replied Mordechai, still unappeased. "Is that why he had to come to your house for an entire *Shabbos*?"

"And what if we are friends?" Levi broke in. "Are you the only friend I'm allowed to have?"

Before the conversation could go any further, it was Mordechai's turn at bat.

After practice, Mordechai seemed apologetic. "Do you want to come over tomorrow after school?" he inquired.

"Sure," Levi replied, relieved to be back on good terms with Mordechai.

Then he remembered. Tomorrow he and Baruch were going to be learning. Maybe I'll cancel learning with Big Baruch, he thought to himself. After all, why ruin an old friendship on account of something that could just as easily be done another time?

But Levi realized guiltily that learning should take first priority. "I'm really sorry, Mordechai," he apologized. "I just remembered that I'm supposed to learn with Baruch tomorrow. Maybe you'd like to come over to prepare with us too. Baruch's really great. You wouldn't believe how much of the *Mishnayos* he knows. I really don't think Baruch would mind."

Mordechai's voice grew cold again. "No thanks, Levi. I like to be careful about the friends I associate with. Big Baruch isn't exactly on the top of my list of potential friends.

"You're my friend," he said more slowly, "but I can't say for how much longer . . . if you continue like this with Big Baruch. After all, one can judge people by the company they choose to keep. I think you'll have to decide exactly in whose company you prefer to be." With that, Mordechai turned away.

It was clear to Levi that he might be gaining one friend only to lose another. He hoped Mordechai would forget about the whole thing by tomorrow. After all, he thought, he and I have been friends for years. He wouldn't let a little thing like this get between us, would he?

MR. SIMONS WALKED INTO CLASS ON MONDAY afternoon in an obviously good mood. The boys all groaned inwardly. They knew what Mr. Simons' good moods meant—more work for them in the form of another of his infamous math problems. The incident with the computers seemed to have done nothing to put a damper on Mr. Simons' desire to challenge his class.

It didn't take him long to prove them correct. "I'll give you the rest of class time to work on this," he announced. "You can do this either by your-selves or in groups of two. The right answer will be worth a bonus of fifty points on your final grade."

Most of the boys got up to find themselves partners. Levi and Mordechai usually paired off for such assignments. Levi was a little hesitant about approaching Mordechai after the incident on the ball field, but for fifty points, he was willing to swallow his pride. He headed towards Mordechai's desk.

Mordechai glanced up at Levi, but seemed to look right through him. He got up and brushed past Levi, stopping at another boy's desk.

"*Nu*, Dovid," Mordechai initiated, loud enough for Levi to hear, "how about being my partner?"

"Sounds good to me," Dovid agreed. Mordechai pulled his chair over and sat down to work.

Levi felt his face burning. He wasn't about to let Mordechai get the better of him. If this is how Mordechai wants to be, who needs him anyway? Levi thought angrily.

He looked over towards Big Baruch's seat. He was alone, as Levi had expected, and had already started the problem. Levi went over to his desk.

"Would you like to work on the problem together?" he asked, pulling over a chair.

Baruch glared at Levi. "No, I actually wouldn't, Newman," he said loud enough to cause most of the heads in the classroom to turn. "Why don't you just leave me alone. I don't need your help. I like working alone. Just go do it without me!"

With that outburst, Big Baruch reached out to

push away the chair that Levi had pulled over. Unfortunately, he didn't notice that Mr. Simons was coming up the aisle to see what all the commotion was about.

Big Baruch sent the chair sailing down the aisle . . . right into Mr. Simons. Mr. Simons was none too pleased at being hit with a chair, especially one moving with the force which only Big Baruch could muster.

"It's a good thing you do like to work alone, Baruch," he said with sarcasm, "because that's just what you'll get to do." Baruch spent his math hour working on the problem outside the principal's office until the principal had time to see him.

As for Levi, he never did earn the fifty bonus points for solving Mr. Simons' problem. He was much too upset trying to solve his own problems. First the incident with Mordechai, and now this, he thought miserably. I've had enough of this kind of treatment from the two of them. The next move will have to be one of theirs. I certainly don't need to be humiliated by either one of them again.

"See you around, Levi," Dovid called with a smirk as he, Shimmy and Mordechai left school. Shimmy waved a farewell, but Mordechai didn't say a word.

Levi ignored them and waited in front of the school for a while to see if Big Baruch would show up as they had planned, but there was no sign of him.

Probably changed his mind, Levi grumbled as he headed for home. I don't know what got into me, asking Big Baruch to learn with me. I'm much better off without him, if that's the way he wants to be.

Once home, Levi proceeded directly upstairs to start on his homework. Chaim stopped him in the upstairs hallway.

"Where's Baruch? Didn't you say he was coming today to learn with you?"

"Sorry, Chaim, I don't think he can make it," said Levi, closing the door to his room.

"I'll watch in case he comes," Chaim called through the closed door. He ran down the steps and planted himself by the window.

An hour later, Levi finished his homework and decided to begin the *Mishnayos* review on his own. A mere five minutes later, he closed the *Mishnayos* with exasperation, in desperate need of some assistance.

"Levi, Levi, I see him!" Chaim shouted from the top of the steps. "Baruch is coming. He's outside now."

Levi opened his door and looked out at Chaim. "Calm down, Chaim. Even if you saw him, that doesn't mean he's coming here. He does happen to live three blocks away, so you'll see him a lot of times when you look outside. Now why don't you just go back downstairs and . . ."

Levi's words were interrupted by the sound of

the doorbell ringing. Chaim flew down the steps and threw open the door.

"Levi said you weren't coming, but I knew you were," Chaim rambled excitedly. "I even saw you outside. Do you want to play with my truck again?"

"Maybe later," Baruch replied. "Right now I need to learn with Levi. I'm a little late, though. Is he here?"

"He's upstairs in his room," Chaim explained.

"Actually, I think he's right behind you," said Baruch as Levi came down the steps. "Why don't you go find your truck now so you'll know where it is in case I have time later?"

Chaim ran off happily.

"Hi," said Levi sheepishly. "I guess you decided to show up after all."

"Well, better late than never, right?" said Baruch. "If there's one thing I'm good for, it's keeping my word, and I did say I would learn with you today after school. Sorry I'm late. Remember how I got sent to the principal by Simons?"

"How could I forget?" Levi asked.

"Well, the principal decided that I could stay an extra hour after school and clean up Simons' room, since I had such a lack of regard for *yeshivah* furniture."

"Sorry you got stuck like that," Levi said.

"Actually, I'm sorry for what happened in class," Baruch replied. "I just think we need to make things clear right from the start. I don't need any favors from anyone."

"Well," said Levi with a wry smile, "that makes one of us. I certainly do need a favor from you, so could you come upstairs so we can get started on the *Mishnayos*? I've been breaking my teeth on this one *Mishnah*. I don't know what I would have done if you hadn't come."

The two boys headed upstairs and spent an hour engrossed in their learning.

"Shall we learn again next week?" Levi inquired after they had finished.

"I think if we expect to finish all of the *Mishnayos* in time for the test, we'd better make it twice a week," Baruch replied.

"Fine with me," Levi said. "Are Mondays and Wednesdays okay?"

"Fine," said Baruch. He got up to leave.

"Thanks for coming," Levi said. "I think it went well."

Baruch didn't reply. If he had benefitted from their learning together, it seemed he wasn't about to admit it.

He was stopped by Chaim on his way out and played with Chaim and his truck for several minutes before leaving.

Wednesday's learning went well, as did the next few sessions. But any attempts by Levi to engage Big Baruch in friendly conversation, either before or after the learning, were always cut short abruptly by Big Baruch.

"Would you like to stay for supper?" Levi had asked casually one night.

"I told you, Newman, I don't need favors. Don't try to push any on me, okay?"

Levi tried not to feel insulted. But why won't Baruch open up to me, he wondered? Why do I even try? I guess I'll just stick to learning with him and forget about anything else.

The next day, Levi was struggling to carry his science project to school. "I'll help you with that," said a familiar voice from behind.

"That's all right, Baruch," said Levi with a hint of sarcasm. "I think I can manage without any favors from you."

"What do you mean?" Big Baruch questioned. "You're not going to get that to school in one piece the way you're going right now."

Levi decided that he had to let Baruch know what was really bothering him. "Well, why is it that it's okay for me to accept favors from you, but you won't take any from me?" he asked.

Levi stole a sidelong glance at Baruch to see his reaction. Big Baruch didn't look angry.

"I don't know, Newman," came the surprising reply. "I guess I just never thought about it. Maybe a favor or two isn't that bad from some people. I guess you have a point."

"Well, in that case, can you take this side for me? I think you're right. I'll never get this to school in one piece without you!"

"Thanks a lot for your help," Levi panted when they had deposited the project on the table next to the others.

"It's the least I could do to help out my *chavrusa*," Big Baruch mumbled as he left the room.

With all the time we're spending learning together, maybe something is finally happening, Levi thought with wonder. It certainly isn't anything like what I had with Mordechai, but it's a start.

Mordechai's friendship already seemed a thing of the past.

SINCE MORDECHAI WALKED HOME THE SAME way as Levi, he couldn't help but notice that Big Baruch accompanied Levi home twice a week. Not to be outdone, he made it his business to have friends over twice a week as well.

"Hey, isn't that Levi across the street?" Shmully asked one day as he walked home beside Mordechai. "Who's he walking with? It isn't . . . I mean it couldn't be . . . Big Baruch, is it?"

"Sure is, Shmully," Mordechai replied.

"Well, what's this world coming to, anyway?" Shmully gasped. "First they show up together that one *Shabbos* at your house, and now they're going home together. I thought Big Baruch was out to get Levi. Now they're friends?"

"I don't understand it either," Mordechai sighed. "I asked Levi about it, and he said they were just learning together to prepare for the *Mishnayos* test. He hasn't spoken to me since."

Shmully couldn't believe it. "What? You and Levi aren't speaking? But you've been friends for ages. Nothing like this ever happened to you two before. What's come over Levi, anyway?"

"I wish I knew," said Mordechai.

"We've got to do something," Shmully said, shaking his head. "We've got to talk some sense into him. Getting prepared for a *Mishnayos* test can drive any of us to drastic measures, but learning with that bully? I never would have believed it if I hadn't seen it with my own eyes."

"I told Levi that people judge you by who you spend time with," explained Mordechai. "I guess he doesn't care."

"Well, if he doesn't care, you've got to," Shmully replied excitedly. "He's your best friend. You've got to remind him who he's dealing with. How can you let him slip away like that?"

"I told you, I already tried to talk to him," said an exasperated Mordechai. "I don't want to speak *lashon hara*, so let's just drop this."

"This is not an issue of *lashon hara*. It's an issue of *hatzalah*. We certainly are allowed to say and do anything to help save Levi from someone like Big Baruch, who would be a terrible influence on him. How could he forget so fast what Big Baruch did in the past? We've got to do more than talk to him, if that already failed. We've got to show him, remind him who he's dealing with."

"I guess you're right, but how?" Mordechai began to mumble aloud the beginnings of a plan which was taking shape in his mind. "I think I have an idea."

"You do?"

"Yeah. Remember the Levi the Tailor incident? We'll just remind Levi about it."

"How?" Shmully inquired.

"Like this," answered Mordechai.

They both sat down on Mordechai's front porch. Shmully peered over Mordechai's shoulder while he wrote:

Due to the great demand for the tailoring talents noted after our previous advertisement, Levi the Tailor is making a comeback! Don't miss this grand opportunity for:

TAILORING BY LEVI
No job too small!
Mending . . . Sewing . . . Tailoring . . .
Fast and efficient service
Competitive rates!

"What's that going to do?" Shmully asked after reading the flyer.

"We want to remind Levi that Big Baruch started up with him in the first place," explained Mordechai. "Levi will come to his senses real quick and drop Baruch once he remembers whose fault this whole thing is, even if it takes something drastic to remind him."

"You mean he'll think Baruch made the flyer this time too?" Shmully asked. "How do you know he'll blame Baruch?"

"Because Baruch did it the first time," Mordechai explained. "Why wouldn't he do the same thing again? This is certainly worth a shot, don't you think? How else can we show Levi that his new *chavrusa* isn't a good influence?"

"What if Big Baruch finds out we did it?" Shmully asked, suddenly afraid.

"How will he ever find out?" Mordechai replied. "We'll hang up copies in the *yeshivah* tonight when it's open for night *shiurim*. No one will ever find out."

Shmully still looked worried. "Look at it this way," Mordechai continued. "If it works, then we've helped Levi. If not, we've fulfilled our *achrayis* to warn Levi who he's dealing with."

"I guess so," said Shmully.

"Good," said Mordechai. "Then I'll just rewrite the flyer neatly and we'll go make some copies at the store."

Presently, Mordechai was finished. "Ready?" Shmully asked.

"In a minute," said Mordechai. "Let me just tell my mother where we're going."

"Mom," Mordechai opened the door and called into the house. "I'm going to the store to make some copies with Shmully."

"Mordechai, could you please take Yehuda with you?" his mother asked. "He's been dying to go out all day, and I just haven't had the chance to take him."

"Fine with me," Mordechai replied. He helped his younger brother on with his coat, and they left together with Shmully.

Yehuda skipped alongside Mordechai. "Where are we going?" he asked.

"To the store to copy some papers," Mordechai replied.

"For what?"

"For a friend of mine," Mordechai replied.

"Oh, you mean Levi?" asked Yehuda.

"Who said anything about Levi?" Mordechai responded. "I certainly have other friends, you know."

"Then who's it for?" Yehuda asked.

"It is for Levi," said Mordechai, somewhat flustered. "But it's a surprise for him so he can't see it until tomorrow."

Yehuda giggled, happy to be included in a surprise. He was even more pleased when

Mordechai gave him a turn to push the button on the copy machine. He insisted on keeping the copy he had produced himself.

"Why don't I just hang these up tonight myself?" offered Shmully on the way back to Mordechai's house. "My father goes to *shiur* tonight at the *yeshivah*. I'll just go with him, and you can stay home if you want."

"It's fine with me, if you can handle it yourself," agreed Mordechai. "I was wondering how I was going to convince my mother to let me go over to the *yeshivah* tonight."

"Can I come?" asked Yehuda. "I'll hang up mine."

"No, Yehuda," Mordechai explained. "I just said I wasn't going, so you're not either."

"See you tomorrow," Mordechai waved as Shmully headed for home.

"I'm glad you're back," greeted Mordechai's mother when they came in. "While you were gone, a friend came to play with you, Yehuda."

"I'm going upstairs to do my homework now," Mordechai called over his shoulder. Yehuda ran into the playroom to find his friend, who, as he hoped, was Chaim Newman.

"How come you came?" Yehuda asked as they sat down to play with matchbox cars.

"My mother had to go to the dentist," Chaim replied.

"Couldn't you stay home with Levi?"

"No, he's busy learning with Baruch. Mommy didn't want me to bother them. She said she'd be back soon to get me. I guess she's probably on her way now, because you were gone for so long. Where were you?"

"It's a surprise," Yehuda whispered confidentially.

"Surprise for who?" Chaim whispered back.

"For Mordechai's friend," Yehuda replied.

"Oh, for Levi?" Chaim guessed. "Tell me! I promise I won't tell Levi. I like surprises."

"Well, he's not supposed to know until tomorrow," began Yehuda, feeling very self-important. "That's what Mordechai and Shmully said. Shmully is going to go hang them up at the *yeshivah* tonight. I helped make the surprise. Here it is."

Yehuda showed Chaim the piece of paper he had helped copy. Both boys bent their heads over the paper to study it closely, neither wanting to admit he had no idea what it was all about.

"Do you think he'll like the surprise?" Yehuda asked Chaim.

"Of course," answered Chaim. "Doesn't everybody like surprises?"

"You can keep this," said Yehuda, handing Chaim the paper. "Just remember, Levi can't see it until tomorrow."

"Okay," said Chaim, stuffing the paper into his pocket.

Just then, Mrs. Newman arrived. "Chaim, it's

time to go," she called from the doorway. "Say thank you and let's go. If we hurry, maybe you'll even get to see Baruch before he leaves. He promised he'd build a block tower with you if we're home in time."

Chaim hurried out the door beside his mother.

They arrived just as Baruch finished learning with Levi. "I see you made it," Baruch said to Chaim. "I was hoping you would, because I don't have any blocks at home, and I wanted to use yours."

"You can come play with them anytime," Chaim declared, following Baruch into the family room. "Where's Levi?" he asked.

"He's upstairs doing homework," Baruch answered.

"Did Mordechai tell you about the surprise?" asked Chaim, curious to find out what it was really all about.

"What surprise?" asked Baruch absently, busy selecting red blocks for a tower.

"The surprise that he and Shmully made," Chaim said.

"What is it?" urged Baruch, suddenly interested. "If you tell me, I can tell you if I know about it."

"Well, I can't tell you," said Chaim, "but I can show you."

He pulled out the crumpled piece of paper from his pocket. "You won't tell Levi, right, not until tomorrow?" Chaim said before handing it to Baruch.

"Of course not," answered Baruch. He quickly scanned the paper.

"Mordechai gave you this?" he asked.

"No, Yehuda did. He said Shmully is going to hang up more copies at the *yeshivah* tonight. Do you think that Levi will like the surprise?"

"I'm sure it will be some surprise, all right," Baruch replied. He had quickly guessed that the flyer must have something to do with ruining the relationship that Levi and he had established. "I'm not quite sure who will be surprised, though," he added.

Chaim nodded intelligently, still unsure what was going on. Baruch handed Chaim back his paper and continued building his tower.

SHMULLY AND MORDECHAI WERE AMONG THE first to enter the school building the next morning. They soon realized, however, that they hadn't come early enough. No matter how hard they looked, they couldn't find any trace of the flyers they had made up.

"I thought you said you could handle hanging up the flyers on your own," Mordechai said accusingly.

"Honest, I hung them all up last night," Shmully replied.

"Then where are they?" Mordechai snapped,

peering into a garbage can near the bulletin board. "Who could have taken them all down so quickly?"

"What if Big Baruch found out?" Shmully asked nervously, looking over his shoulder as if expecting to see Big Baruch looming behind him.

"Don't be silly," said Mordechai. "How could Big Baruch have found out? No, there has to be some reasonable explanation for all of this."

Neither of the boys could come up with one, though.

When Levi arrived home after school, Chaim was waiting for him at the door. He was going to take one more stab at trying to discover what the surprise had been all about. "So, did you like the surprise?" he inquired.

"What surprise?" Levi replied, heading into the kitchen for a snack.

"The surprise at school today," said Chaim in an exasperated tone.

"I don't know what you're talking about," Levi said, only half listening as he mixed himself a glass of chocolate milk.

"The surprise that Mordechai and Shmully made for you," Chaim pressed.

Levi put down his glass of chocolate milk.

"Can you just tell me what you're talking about?" he implored, finally giving his brother his full attention.

"Did you have so many surprises today that

you can't remember which one I mean?" asked Chaim, amazed at his brother's apparent denseness. He fished in his pocket for the piece of paper Yehuda had given him. "This surprise. Did you like it? What is it, anyway?"

Levi read the paper. Indeed, he looked quite surprised, even shocked. "It's a great surprise Chaim, just great," he said shakily.

"So you liked it, right? Baruch said you would be surprised when I showed it to him."

"Where did you get it?" Levi questioned, confused. "I thought you just said it was from Mordechai. What does Baruch have to do with it?"

"I showed it to Baruch yesterday after Yehuda gave it to me. Yehuda helped Shmully and Mordechai make them, and then Shmully went to the *yeshivah* last night to hang them up for you. I bet it looked nice when you got there this morning."

"Yeah, it was a wonderful surprise," murmured Levi, thinking. Exactly what had happened was still uncertain, but one thing that appeared clear was that in Baruch he had gained a friend, one who had saved him from another embarrassing situation.

Levi didn't mention the incident to Baruch the next day. Baruch also refrained from bringing it up, so Levi was still not one hundred percent sure if he had guessed right about where he stood with Baruch.

Several days later, Levi found himself practically dragged to the back of the playground by none other than Big Baruch. Instantly, Levi was sure that he must have misjudged their relationship, which had seemed to improve so much in the last few weeks.

Now what? Levi wondered. Don't I deserve better treatment than this from Baruch? He felt the familiar pounding of his heart as he stood alone with Big Baruch, their faces only inches apart.

"You've got to help me, Newman," Baruch said, clenching and unclenching his fists nervously in his characteristic gesture. He released his grip on Levi to reveal, just as on that day which now seemed ages ago, a split in his pants. Levi tried hard to stifle the urge to laugh as he viewed Big Baruch's head upside down peering at him between his massive legs.

Once again, Levi had to forego his lunch in order to help Baruch. This time, he wasn't nearly as nervous.

"Let's not make a habit of this," Levi teased Baruch.

"Well, it's not like I do it on purpose, you know," Baruch replied defensively. "But don't worry. I'm going to repay you for all you've done somehow, Levi . . . and I don't just mean fixing my pants."

Baruch noticed Levi's suddenly wary glance. "Awww, don't worry, Newman," he smirked. "I wouldn't do anything like before. I just feel like I owe you a lot."

"What are you talking about?" Levi replied. "If anyone owes, it's me, for all the time you've spent with me on the *Mishnayos* test. You don't seem to realize how much you've helped me. So it appears that I owe you, too."

Levi grew thoughtful. "Maybe our friendship is adequate payment for both of us," he mused.

Baruch nodded his head in agreement and gave Levi an approving slap on the back. It sent Levi reeling across the room, but Baruch managed to catch him before he fell. The boys laughed together, feeling like they had made a real connection.

"Where were you, Levi?" Shimmy asked mockingly when he saw Levi in the hall near the end of lunch hour.

Levi and Baruch had just returned from Levi's house. They had hoped that no one would miss them, but clearly this was not the case.

"Off with your good buddy Big Baruch again?" jeered Dovid. "Don't you like our company any more?" Mordechai stood nearby, looking rather uncomfortable.

Levi, feeling outnumbered, tried to push past the boys. He still had about ten minutes left of lunch time and wanted to have something to eat before the next class. But the other boys didn't let him pass.

Levi realized that Mordechai was not the ring-leader. It was just too out of character. For Dovid and Shimmy, however, it was a definite possibility.

"I see now, Mordechai, that you were right," Levi said softly. "It seems you really can judge a person by the company he keeps."

Mordechai flushed, but the comment went right over Dovid and Shimmy's heads, and they continued to needle Levi.

"Where's your good friend, anyway?" Dovid asked with mock concern.

His concern turned quite real when he received his answer. "I'm right behind you, Dovid," growled Big Baruch. He had come looking for Levi after getting both their lunch bags from the classroom.

Levi watched the color drain from Dovid's face as he, Shimmy and Mordechai backed away from Levi to let him pass. However, Big Baruch had no intention of letting the three off the hook that easily. Levi noticed the now familiar sign of Baruch's emotional turmoil, the clenching and unclenching of his fists, as the lunch bags lay forgotten at his feet.

But Levi was not about to let Baruch get into trouble if he could help it. He grabbed Baruch's elbow and tried to lead him towards the classroom door.

"Let go of me, Newman," Big Baruch said with annoyance, easily shaking Levi off. "Sometimes people need to get what they deserve."

"Come on, Baruch." Levi tried stepping between Baruch and the others. "We don't have much time left if we want to have any lunch before our next class. Why waste time on them, anyway?"

Big Baruch, not used to controlling his emotions, looked past Levi to Dovid, Shimmy and Mordechai. His eyes then rested on the lunch bags.

"Maybe you're right, Newman," he finally agreed. "Let's go have lunch.

After another threatening look at the threesome, Baruch turned around. He headed out the door towards the playground, followed by Levi.

Mordechai, Shimmy and Dovid were relieved to be left alone. But Dovid felt like he had to save face.

"It looks to me like Big Baruch the so-called Bully is turning into a bit of a coward now," he said.

Mordechai just glared at him and stalked off down the hall alone. Levi's statement about the friends he had picked had really hit home.

Mordechai was not in the best of moods when he arrived home later that afternoon. Eli, his older brother, came home a short time afterwards.

"How about going outside to play some basketball?" Eli asked cheerfully.

Usually, such an invitation from Eli would be

welcomed by Mordechai, since with a full *yeshivah* schedule, Eli didn't have much time to spend with his brother. This time, however, Mordechai was just not in the mood.

"No thanks," he mumbled.

"Why not?" Eli asked. "Since when do you refuse a game of basketball? I'll tell you what, I'll even give you a head start. How about ten points to get you going? I guarantee I'll still beat you!"

"Not today, okay, Eli? I'd rather be left alone."

Eli looked at him sharply. "What's up, Mordechai?" he asked softly. "I bet this has something to do with Levi. I haven't seen him around here in a while. I don't recall you going to his house lately, either."

"Why does everyone around here think about Levi so much?" Mordechai snapped. "Can't a guy just take a little break and hang out with different people sometimes?"

"Sure, Mordechai, but isn't Levi your best friend?" Eli asked pointedly.

"Was, you mean," Mordechai mumbled.

"Want to talk about it?" Eli asked, sitting down next to Mordechai.

"There's nothing to say, really," replied Mordechai. "One day he was my friend, and the next thing I knew, he was hanging around with Big Baruch. They've been preparing for the *Mishnayos* test together, and that doesn't seem to leave Levi much time for me."

"Why don't you just tell them you'd like to join them? That way you could spend time with Levi, and I bet it would be a great way for you to prepare for the test, too."

"Learn with them? I said he's learning with Big Baruch. You know who Big Baruch is, don't you?"

Eli nodded. Even the seventh-graders were well aware of Big Baruch's reputation. Eli looked thoughtful for a moment.

"I have heard of Big Baruch, but I also know Levi. I can't imagine Baruch's as bad as he's made out to be if Levi's willing to spend time learning *Mishnayos* with him. Maybe Levi sees something in Big Baruch that we're all missing. What do you think?"

"I already told Levi what I think," said Mordechai bitterly. "I told him it's either Big Baruch or me. I told him I'm not about to spend time with the likes of Big Baruch, and if he wants to keep doing it, he isn't going to pull me down with him."

"But Levi's your best friend!" said Eli emphatically. "You can't just drop him like that."

"What do you mean?" retorted Mordechai. "Levi's the one who dropped me for Big Baruch."

"Well," Eli said, "you know Levi better than I do. Didn't you always consider him to be a reasonable person?"

"I just don't know, Eli," Mordechai explained. "Levi, of all people, told me today that my friends were pulling me down. Here he is, spending all this time with the likes of Big Baruch, and he has the nerve to tell me I should be careful about my friends. I just don't get him."

"Look, I don't know anything about these other friends, but I do know Levi," said Eli. "He's a good guy. At least you owe him a chance to prove that he isn't making the mistake you think he is. Who knows? Maybe he's right, and you're wrong. Maybe it's your friends that aren't as wonderful as you think, not Baruch."

Mordechai looked pensive. "I don't know, Eli. Everyone's always known all about Big Baruch. But maybe you're right. I shouldn't just drop Levi without even giving him a chance. I'll think about it. Maybe after the *Mishnayos* test I'll see if we can get back together."

Eli looked pleased.

"Now," Eli said with a smile, "how about that game of basketball?"

"Sure thing," Mordechai answered. "But keep your extra ten points. You're going to need them!"

14

ON WEDNESDAY, LEVI AND BARUCH PLANNED TO study together as usual. Levi's mother was making an after-school *siyum* at home for one of her classes. The boys had no intention of being around when there was a chance of so many girls being on the same premises.

They decided that with the *Mishnayos* test coming up so soon, they would learn at Baruch's house instead of skipping their regular Wednesday session. Up until now, they had learned exclusively at Levi's house. This had never bothered Levi, and Baruch had never even suggested that they go to his house.

When the two boys got to Baruch's house, they climbed up the three steps and onto the front porch. Before Baruch had a chance to turn the knob, the door was flung open, and a woman who could only be Baruch's mother gestured them inside.

"Baruch, *baybaleh*," she cooed, pinching his cheek. "I'm so glad you're home and with such a nice friend, too."

She looked Levi up and down as if to check whether he was indeed good enough for her Baruch.

"So, *zeeskeit*," she continued, putting her arm around Baruch and leading him further into the house. "Is this the Levi fellow who Tatti tells me you've been kind enough to spend so much of your precious time learning with? You really are a *malachel*. Isn't he?" she asked, glancing Levi's way.

Levi nodded, but Baruch's mother turned her attentions back to Baruch without noticing. Levi found himself completely overwhelmed by Baruch's mother. He imagined that Baruch probably was, too. Baruch seemed to shrink inside himself at her presence, unable to even get a word in edgewise.

"You boys must be simply ravenous after such a long day at school," Baruch's mother stated with certainty. "Aren't you?"

She didn't wait for any reply. She led them to

the kitchen and set before each of them the biggest piece of chocolate cake Levi had ever been served.

"Now tell me all about your day while you eat, *faygeleh*," she urged Baruch.

Before Baruch could swallow what was in his mouth to reply, the answer had already been provided. "You did wonderfully as usual, right? I'll never forget the exciting phone call from your *rebbe* to your father and me just the other day. He called just to let us know what a *tzaddikel* my little *yingeleh* is and how well you're doing in class. Not that I had ever imagined otherwise, but it is nice to hear another's opinion sometimes, now isn't it?"

Levi wondered if she realized what she had just said. It was quite clear that the only opinion that ever mattered to her was her own!

As soon as they finished their cake, the two boys escaped upstairs to Baruch's room. With an almost audible sigh of relief, Baruch closed the door behind them, and the boys began learning.

When they had finished and tucked their *Mishnayos* back into their backpacks, Levi looked at Baruch's troubled face.

"What's up?" he asked softly.

Baruch looked down at his hands, which were clenched tightly into fists in his lap.

"I just wanted to say thanks," he said in a quiet but firm voice. "Thanks for being my first real friend."

Levi maintained an uneasy silence, and Baruch continued. "You can't imagine what it's like to never have had any friends. I guess I just accepted that I didn't have anything to offer a friend. I wasn't about to let anyone know how much it really bothered me.

"The thing that bothered me the most was being a nobody," Baruch continued sadly. "I fixed that problem by earning my infamous reputation as a class bully. It did earn me status, though I sure didn't earn any friends that way. It wasn't until you came along and showed me that I really had something to offer that I felt I could be a worthwhile friend. That's what I wanted you to know, Levi. Thanks again."

Levi was rather overwhelmed. He was not sure how to respond. He just nodded his head and bent over his backpack as if to tighten the straps. When he straightened up, he found Baruch's eyes still on him and knew a reply was expected.

"You know, Baruch, I've gained a lot from you too," Levi explained. "Besides all the *Mishnayos* help, I mean. I've learned that when you are dealing with people, there's always more than meets the eye."

Baruch grinned. He understood what Levi meant. The two boys walked downstairs in companionable silence. Baruch opened the door for Levi. The squeak of the door brought Baruch's mother in an instant.

"Good-bye, Levi," she said with a cheery wave, wrapping her arm possessively around her son. "We must have him again soon, right, darling? Yes, do come again soon."

Levi walked the few blocks home engrossed in his thoughts. Now that he had seen Baruch at home, everything about him made sense.

Levi thought back to when he had met Baruch in first grade. Baruch had been the only new face in their class. The rest of the class had already been together for two years. Baruch's mother had kept him home until that year. Perhaps she had been so protective of him because he was an only child.

In his mind's eye, Levi was back in first grade seeing Baruch for the first time. He remembered just how the conversation had gone.

"What's his name?" Mordechai had whispered to Levi.

"How should I know?" Levi had replied. "I think I've seen him at *shul,* but he's never come to my house to play."

"Look how tall he is," marveled Dovid, the shortest boy in the class.

"Maybe he's really in the wrong class," snickered Shimmy.

They all had murmured in agreement as they huddled together in their group, leaving Baruch standing alone, pretending to examine the bulletin board.

Baruch had been quite aware that the boys were talking about him. The long stares and loud whispers made that obvious to anyone. He had just pretended not to care. His cheeks were flushed red, but his head was held high. If these were the boys his mother had thought would be his friends, he wanted no part of them. Instead of learning how to make friends, Baruch had used his extra size to become a bully.

Going over what Baruch had just told him in his room, Levi understood how much difficulty Baruch had had with each step of their developing friendship. Baruch's relationship with his mother clearly hadn't helped, either. He wasn't foolish enough to believe all the praise she showered on him, but he had a very hard time seeing himself objectively.

At least Baruch was finally coming around, Levi thought. Who would have guessed that so much would evolve from the silly Levi the Tailor incident? Who would have guessed that Levi the Tailor would find a true friend in Big Baruch the Bully?

15

THE DAY OF THE BIG *MISHNAYOS* TEST ARRIVED. All the boys in the class exchanged nervous glances as they came in that morning. Some sat down at their desks to take a last minute glimpse at the *Mishnah* before the test. Most joined the sizable crowd that gathered in the back of the room.

"Someone tell me what this *Mishnah* means!" Shmully pleaded, holding out his *Mishnah* in front of the nose of anyone within reach.

They all waved him away. Explaining anything to a frantic Shmully right before a test was known to be an impossible task.

"Did anyone get all the answers to questions fifty-nine through sixty-three on the review sheet?" asked someone else.

A few boys attempted to provide answers, and more and more last minute questions were pelted back and forth.

"Reb Hirsh is here," wailed Shmully, seeing his last chance of having the *Mishnah* explained disappear.

Reb Hirsh walked in with a stack of test papers tucked under his arm. The boys headed for their seats in silence. Baruch looked back at Levi and they exchanged weak smiles to wish each other luck.

The test was the grueling experience they had all expected, though some were obviously better prepared than others. At first, only the scratching of pencils could be heard, but soon a few sighs of hopelessness came from some of the boys, especially from Shmully's direction.

"You are going to be grading on a curve this time, aren't you?" he asked hopefully.

Reb Hirsh didn't answer. He just put his finger to his lips to signal silence. It was quiet for a few more minutes until Shmully, unable to bear it any longer, broke the silence again.

"I just can't do it, Rebbe," he moaned. "Will there at least be a make-up test?"

This time, Reb Hirsh motioned him out into the

hall to talk, leaving the door open in case he was needed. Another boy got up and went over to the door.

"I think I'm sick, Rebbe," he said with a mock grimace of pain. "My stomach's been hurting me all morning. Maybe I should go home."

Reb Hirsh put his arm around him and firmly guided him back to his seat.

"Just finish the test," he said. "I'm sure you'll feel much better when you're through." He also guided Shmully back to his seat and asked him to finish as best as he could.

Levi was too busy trying to fill out all of the answers he could in the allotted time to notice all these occurrences. He had, however, glanced up a few times at Baruch. He saw him bent over his paper writing for all he was worth.

The first boy finished was the one who had spent most of his time sighing: Shmully. In the end, he just gave up, passed in his paper and stomped noisily out of the room. As others finished, they went out one by one to the empty playground.

"Could you believe such a hard test?" Shmully complained. "You'd think we were in *yeshivah gedolah*."

"Well, I didn't even get half of them right," piped up someone else.

"How could he expect us to know so many *Mishnayos*?" complained another.

"Did anyone get the answer to the last question?" Dovid asked.

"The last question; what about the first?" Shimmy asked.

"What about the three part question? Did any of you remember all three parts?" inquired Levi.

"Let's not talk about this any more," moaned Shmully, covering his ears with his hands.

"Well, at least it's over," Levi attempted to comfort him. "We did our best, and that's about the most any Rebbe can ask for." The boys all nodded in agreement.

Levi felt a tap on his shoulder. Mordechai motioned him over to the side.

"Now that the test is over," Mordechai initiated in a low voice, "maybe you want to come over and shoot some baskets at my house after school?"

Levi looked pleasantly surprised. "How about you come to my house instead?" he asked cheerfully. "You know my driveway's wider than yours. Besides . . ."—he paused, looking uncomfortable—"I've already invited Baruch over after school. Maybe he'll show us that great jump shot he used yesterday at recess."

"Okay," Mordechai answered reluctantly. He was not about to give up on reconciling with Levi after making the first move. "I'll meet you after school."

Levi agreed, looking pleased. He went to look for Baruch.

"Baruch," he said, "I just wanted to let you know that Mordechai's coming over this afternoon to play basketball with us. You don't mind, do you?"

"You know my opinion of your friends, Newman," Baruch replied with an automatic scowl. Then his expression softened. "As I've told you before, though, I'm a man of my word. I promised to teach you that jump shot I used yesterday, so I guess I'll be there."

"Great!" Levi said. "I'll meet you right after school."

When school was over, Mordechai and Levi waited at the door for Baruch. Dovid and Shimmy passed by.

"Hey, Mordechai," Dovid called. "Want to come over and celebrate surviving the *Mishnayos* test with us?"

"No thanks," Mordechai answered firmly. Dovid shrugged his shoulders as he and Shimmy walked past.

Baruch arrived a few moments later. As he headed down the school steps with Levi and Mordechai, Shmully raced out the door. He stopped in his tracks in surprise.

"Hey!" he stated to no one in particular. "Mordechai and Levi. It looks like they're back together again. That's great!" Then he took a closer look.

"Wait!" he said in amazement. "Who's that with

them? It couldn't be . . . I mean, it isn't . . . it can't be . . . Big Baruch, can it?"

He watched in amazement as the threesome disappeared around the bend.

"Who would have believed it?"

Glossary

Aishes Chayil: woman of valor

bar-mitzvah: halachic adulthood

bentch: to recite the Grace after Meals

ben Torah: Torah observer

bracha (brachos): blessing(s)

chasunah: wedding

chavrusa: study partner

chesed: kindness

dan lekaf zchus: giving the benefit of the doubt

Gemara: part of the Talmud

hakaros hatov: gratification

hatzalah: emergency rescue team

lashon hara: slander

Maariv: evening prayers

midos: character traits

Mishnah (Mishnayos): part of the Talmud

rebbi: Torah teacher

rosh yeshivah: dean

sefer: book

Shabbos: the Sabbath

shalosh seudos: third *Shabbos* meal

shiur: lecture

shul: synagogue

siyum: conclusion

tichel: kerchief

tznius: modesty

yarmulka: skullcap

yeshivah: Torah school

yeshivah gedolah: Torah high school

yingeleh: little boy

zemer (zemiros): song(s)